I LOVE YOU, I HATE YOU, I MISS YOU

L A MICHAELS

LML Books

OTHER BOOKS BY L A MICHAELS

BETWEEN HEAVEN AND HELL

THE INNOCENT YEARS

NOVELLAS

OUR PRIVATE WORLD APART

For Nikki Baker.
A decade of scheming that started in Kansas ends somewhere epic.

Toto, I have a feeling we're not in Kansas anymore.

- Dorothy, *The Wizard of Oz,* 1939

CONTENTS

PART TWO

PART THREE

PART ONE

CHAPTER ONE

NOAH

Growing up in Kansas was not something that you could easily turn into a five-page college essay. Noah Peters grunted and slammed his laptop shut. He looked into space and returned to reality as he realized he was looking at the wall behind his bedroom desk; the same wall that he had been looking at since birth. The same wall he was destined to look at for the rest of his life. Noah craved change. No one left Wichita, Kansas, though, and if they did, it was for one of the neighboring towns such as Derby or Andover. Possibly, if they were lucky, they would venture to Kansas City, but that was about it. Kansas, the state didn't even have any major sports teams.

Noah's choices growing up were Oklahoma, Missouri, and Texas. He always chose to be a fan of Texas sports. People would try and argue why, but the only reason Noah could think of was that Texas was big. It had Dallas, Houston, and San Antonia, etc. Kansas had corn, wheat, wind, and monopolies no one seemed to talk about.

The blond-haired, brown-eyed tall, tanned by the bright sun boy had gone to the same school his entire life. He had the same friends and the same enemies. A new kid would come to the school very rarely, and after about a week, they started to blend in rather well.

"Wichita can't be my life," Noah said to himself, groaning. There was a knock at the door. "I'm busy," he screamed.

"Mom says it's time for breakfast!" Kelly screamed as she quickly opened the door and then closed it.

The blonde boy sighed and got up from his desk. He was only partially dressed for school but at least had on a shirt, boxer briefs, and socks. He just hadn't gotten around to putting on pants or sneakers yet. "Well, time for another wonderful day…"

* * *

Breakfast at the Peters house was hardly a family affair and hardly a gourmet feast. His mom, Cheryl, worked as a store manager at the local Target. It was sadly one of the nicer stores in town. He didn't mean one of the nicer Target's. They had two. They were both rather clean inside, but the neighborhood Target was definitely a win in terms of places to shop. She was always on the go and always working. Cheryl couldn't keep sales associates to save her life. People would constantly quit their job at Target to do their dream job, which apparently meant going and working at some store at the local mall or something.

His older brother Brick worked as a server at the local Applebee's. He was on his way into management. He had no choice, ever since he got his high school girlfriend Amber pregnant, only a month before they were both supposed to go off to college. They agreed that she would still go, and he would support them. Brick and Amber still hadn't decided whether they would marry or not, but Amber still had six months before the baby was born. Her parents wanted them married. Cheryl was not pushing one way or another. Amber's parents were embarrassed their non-denotational mega-church would find out.

Then there was Kelly, his bratty thirteen-year-old sister. She was a wannabe pageant queen in a family that couldn't afford it. So, she settled on being a cheerleader at the local junior league team. The junior league football team, much like the basketball, baseball, and volleyball (for the girls only, of course), would all start out in the junior league, travel to the middle school, and then be the town's pick for the city high school. There were over five thousand kids. They only accounted for around nine-hundred of them, though, and acted as if it was normal to have a stadium for a football team that hadn't gone to the championships in five years.

Regardless, Kelly was a cheerleader now at the middle school level. Noah had to admit she was good at it, and he was proud of her, but it didn't mean she wasn't a brat. Since Brick knocked up Amber, though, it became his responsibility to take care of Kelly while Cheryl was at work. "I'm going to need you to pick up Kelly from school," Cheryl told her middle child.

Noah looked at her with wide eyes. "I can't! I have a shift at the bookstore," he reminded her. It was the eighth time, as well.

His mother sighed, "Right… Well, Kelly, you are going to have to hitch a ride from a friend's parent or something."

"That's not fair!" Kelly practically screamed.

"Well, you can easily walk. The school is only a twenty-minute walk," Cheryl reminded her daughter.

Kelly crossed her arms and pouted, "Fine. I'll figure it out." She then looked at Noah, "You are doing this just to sabotage me."

Noah had no idea how he was sabotaging her, but it made him smile to think he was. Brick never drove him to and from school growing up. He had to walk most of the time. When they were much younger, Brick had to walk both of his siblings home before being old enough to drive. That was about the bulk of his older sibling helping out. Yet, Noah had to help out with driving and to pick up groceries since he got his car last year. A car that, mind you, he got with his own money that he had been saving for years, "Tough luck, loser."

"Takes one to know one," Kelly bit back.

She wasn't wrong. He was sort of a loser. Noah tended to think he was an outcast in a city full of people who stuck to the status quo with pride. Yet, the only pride he had was in the rainbow flag that he had above his bed. Being gay in the bible belt wasn't exactly something you screamed in the streets. Yes, Noah was indeed out. No, Noah was not the only gay kid at his school. However, he was one of the few out gay kids. That whole saying that guys would often tell him on chat sites pissed him off, like; "*Oh, there are tons of queer kids at your school. They just aren't out yet.*" Well, in this town, they never would be. A senior that he had a brief secret fling with the year before was already engaged to his girlfriend that he had since he was in diapers. Sure, there were queer people, but he rarely ever saw out-and-about couples aside from the rare no-nonsense lesbian couple.

He looked at his phone. "Come on, Kelly. I need to drop you off now, so I'm not late myself." There was only a twenty-minute time difference in their start schedules.

* * *

Wichita West was hard to explain. It was large. It was constantly being expanded for new gyms and other sports-related expenses, but that was about it. It was actually a rather poor school academic wise. They didn't even have books and technically didn't have homework. All students were provided with tablets, but that was part of a four-year-old budget idea that was never fully thought out, as the students could have easily had their textbooks on the tablets, but the school couldn't afford the software. Yet, they had a new sports fundraiser every week.

Noah also didn't have a locker. Well, actually, he did, but he had no idea where it was. He had never seen a kid open a locker in the entire school. There were always rumors they would take lockers out for more trophy cases, but the only trophies they ever got were for baseball and volleyball. The football and basketball teams sucked.

Lily Hamm walked over. She was the closest thing that he had to a friend. Noah knew that technically they were just friends, not close friends, but still. They really didn't hang out after school. "Hey, Noah! Did you finish your college essay?" Lily asked.

"Not yet. I mean, I don't understand the point of writing a college essay for a school that doesn't exist," he explained.

She looked confused as they continued to walk. "I don't understand what you mean. We have to use it to send to Wichita State and KU."

"Yeah, and the essay topic is not on either of their sites. You also do know that you can apply to just about any school you want, right? I mean, you have a 4.0." This was what Noah dreaded. The fact that he knew so many smart kids who never wanted to travel more than fifty miles away for school, only to move right back home after. It seemed so pointless, as half of them ended up working in factories.

"I don't know... I'd rather not risk paying out of state costs," Lily explained. That was the standard answer given by any kid in this school and most in the state, at least in Noah's mind. Before either could say another word, a boy came up to Lily and started to grab her ass. She turned around and started to kiss him. He had a letterman jacket on with the school colors, coral, and orange. The boy happened to be her boyfriend, Ned Ran. Ned was all right looking and was somewhat built, but he wasn't really attractive in the face. At least Noah didn't think so. Lily loved him, but Ned never said he loved her back. In his honest opinion, Lily and Ned were not a match made in heaven. Yet, they would probably end up married after high school.

The bell for the first mod started. His first class was actually volunteering in the counseling office. He somehow got class credit for this. He wasn't entirely sure why but he did. It was mostly just setting up appointments for kids, handing out pamphlets on abstinence, planned parenthood, and why God was always watching. There were no pamphlets on colleges or condoms found in this office though. You know, practical things that one would assume to find in such a place. There were six counselors at the school. His own counselor, Mrs. Barker, was pretty useless. When he had first come out during his freshman year, she had arranged a meeting. She explained that she had no issues with homosexuals but that God might have a different view, and he should worry that some of the other kids might not be as accepting. It essentially ended with her explaining that because he had chosen to come out in high school, it was a verbal contract that any bullying, harassment, or threats that came his way were his own problem. The school would not get involved or side with him. It was a lovely meeting that ended with him in tears in a bathroom stall. Cheryl had bitched the school out, but that didn't really do much in a tone-deaf environment.

Luckily, Noah was rather invisible in the school because of its size. Yet, inevitably, he was always the gay kid, or more eloquently put, the *homosexual*. He wasn't Noah Peters; he wasn't the blond boy; he wasn't Brick's younger brother; he was the gay kid.

Noah sat down at his desk and took out his notebook. He would get some studying done for his math test in the next mod. Not many kids actually used the counseling office, especially not this early on in the fall semester.

The door to Mrs. Barker's office opened up, and the short, plump woman with frizzy brown but graying hair walked out. She was wearing a purple dress that highlighted her large cleavage. Whom was she trying to impress? Noah was still trying to figure that out three years later. A tall, brown-haired boy walked out after her. He had a smile on his face, and Noah couldn't figure out why.

"Noah… Where are Amy and Luna?" Mrs. Barker asked.

He shrugged, "Late? I don't know…" He hadn't seen Amy or Luna since the first day of the semester over a month ago.

The counselor sighed, "Very well… I guess you will have to do this." She said 'you' as if he was the worst of the worst in terms of options. "I need someone to be Timothy's study buddy for the week. I'll line up your schedules as much as possible. I'll have it done by the time you are done giving him the school tour." She grabbed a hall pass and, with reluctance in her eyes, handed it to Noah "I'll expect you back ten minutes before the end of the mod."

Noah wanted to ask if she would attempt to look into why Amy and Luna were not here. He didn't, though. "All right," he said as he looked at Timothy again. Having a name for the boy made him a little bit more attractive for some reason. He needed to snap out of it. He knew better than to look at a guy for a form of attraction. That wasn't how it was done. Noah would get a note to meet a guy in his car at lunchtime where they would kiss, and he would be offered the chance to suck them off. Then he would practically be choked out after they came in his mouth without warning. The choking didn't come from their cum. It came from them, grabbing him tightly and telling him that he couldn't tell anyone. They also said they weren't gay, just horny, and it didn't count because they only kissed for like a second, and Noah sucked their cock, and they didn't touch him.

He shook Timothy's hand and smiled, "Hey. I'm Noah," he explained.

Timothy shook his hand back. He had the strongest grip ever for a rather thin kid. "Nice to meet you! I'm Timothy Powel." He had a deep and sexy voice. Noah once again personally told himself to fuck off. He wasn't allowed to have feelings for guys around here.

"Cool…" That was all the blond boy really could get out. His hand hurt a little bit. He looked at the clock. They had an hour and thirty minutes, and Mrs. Barker wanted them back ten minutes before the end of the mod. "I guess I'll show you around," Noah said.

"Cool!" Timothy said back. It was weird to hear a guy with such a deep voice sound so chipper.

Noah led him outside of the counseling office. He looked around for a minute and decided to go towards the cafeteria. "So, obviously, the cafeteria is in what is essentially the lobby, I guess. You already know where the main office and counseling rooms are. I guess I could show you the library. I'm sure you will want to know where the gym is," Noah said.

"Why do you assume I want to know where the gym is?" Timothy asked.

He didn't really know. It was just an assumption, but most guys did. Plus, Timothy was tall. Most tall guys, regardless of talent, wanted to play basketball. "Oh, I don't know," Noah mumbled.

The brunet haired boy laughed, "Nah, I actually do want to see the gym. I played basketball at my old school."

So, stereotyping paid off for the first and only time ever, "We have four different gyms: the main one where we have pep rallies, and the basketball games. Then the one where they have gym class. We also have a workout style gym. Plus, a volleyball/indoor tennis court gym." The school was currently trying to raise more money for a fifth gym. It was undecided what the gym would be designated for.

"Weird," Timothy stated.

"Oh, definitely, but welcome to Kansas. Or, are you from out of state?" Noah asked. He just kind of assumed he was. He dressed a little to schoolboy prep for Kansas farm boy attire.

"I'm originally from Connecticut. My dad got transferred here for work," he said.

The Peters boy nodded, "Cool. I've lived in this town my entire life," he explained.

Timothy nodded back, "I suppose that is cool," he said as a statement, but Noah questioned if it was actually a question itself. The tall boy looked Noah up and down for a second. "I like your shoes!" he said.

Noah blushed, "Oh, um, thanks. I had to order them. They didn't have them in stock at the mall."

"Yeah. I actually have a pair but in purple at home," Timothy explained.

"So, do you go by Timothy or Tim?" Noah asked.

This made him laugh, "Timothy. Call me anal, but I just like the more formal sounding name. Tim sounds like a guy who works as a manager of a Best Buy. Timothy sounds like a lawyer or a famous person. I don't know. I know it sounds silly."

"You want to be a lawyer, then?" Noah asked.

"Eh… Maybe. Either a lawyer or a doctor. My mom is a lawyer. She isn't practicing right now, though, since we just moved out here. She said she would look back into it after we got settled in," Timothy explained. He had nice deep eyes. Noah couldn't deny it.

"Any siblings?" Noah asked.

"Nope. How about you?" he asked right back.

Noah looked at his phone to make sure that they could make it back to the counseling office with enough time. He also had a little jolt of nerves because he had really wanted to spend this time studying for his math test. He hated that his teacher had scheduled a math test for a Monday. "Oh, I have an older brother and a younger sister," Noah replied. "So, you're the Jan then?" Timothy started laughing.

"The Jan?" Noah asked in complete confusion.

The brown-haired boy laughed again, "Yeah, the Jan Brady. You know, *The Brady Bunch?* It's a classic and just silly fun."

Oh, that is what he meant. Noah thought he was making a gender slur or something for a minute, and he wondered where that would have come from. Had Mrs. Barker mentioned his sexuality? Noah had never come off as being *gay acting*. He totally knew that sounded fucked up to say out loud or even think about, but it was true. If he went to a Pride Parade, then no one would think he was gay. At least Noah didn't think so. He had never been to a Pride event. "I'm not sure if I would be a Jan. I mean, I definitely get the brunt of being the middle child, but I don't know if I complain about it that much." But did he? He was sure that Kelly might argue differently. He and brick had always been relatively close, at least to some degree.

"So, what do you do for fun?" Timothy asked.

There were a lot of *so's* coming out of this kid's mouth. He wasn't sure why. People didn't tend to want to know much about him. He and Lily mostly cracked jokes about their classmates and talked about *The Kardashians.*

"I guess just hang out. I work a lot after school at a local bookstore," Noah replied. Timothy nodded, "Nice. I love to read! Obviously, I love basketball, but I also love music and writing as well."

"You write?... I also write," Noah admitted. He had never told anyone about his writing.

"Oh, really? What about?" the East Coast boy asked.

Noah wasn't prepared to explain his writing to someone, "Just some fiction stuff." As in a gay romance novel about two college-age boys living in California. He had been writing it for years. Noah realized years ago that the stories being written for gay teens and the shows that depicted most queer relationships were rather toxic or way too woke for his taste. He just wanted to read a book where the guys dated, and it was perceived as normal. So, he wrote it himself.

"Well, if you ever want to share any of it, I'd love to read it man," Timothy explained.

This kid didn't even know him. In an hour, he'd be sitting with the jocks in class and making plans for some party at an abandoned barn that weekend where they would all get drunk and pair up with one another. The two of them would probably never speak to one another again. He knew that he was supposed to show him around for the week, but the reality was that the new kid never wanted to stay the new kid for long, and having a tour guide made them feel weird.

"I mean maybe," Noah said to be polite. He looked at his phone again. "Ok, we should get heading back to the counseling office. Mrs. Barker has a stick up her ass for me."

"We didn't make it to the gym, though. Can you maybe show me on your way to your next class?" Timothy asked.

"Oh well, actually, my next class is gym, so yeah, why not?" He had really planned to low-key skip gym to study for the math test, but the math test was just going to be an act of God whether he passed or not.

CHAPTER TWO

TIMOTHY

Timothy couldn't lie. He really didn't feel comfortable at this school so far. Mrs. Barker was kind of a bitch, and Noah confirmed it. She had this don't blame the school or me for any problems that you have attitude. Which was the worst kind of attitude that a school counselor could have. He missed his friends and the rest of his family back home. Noah seemed nice but also stubborn. Every time Timothy asked him a question, he would get all freaked out or act like it was too much for him. He realized that Noah was getting a little fast as they walked to the gym. "Hey, Noah, wait up!" Timothy ran over.

Noah looked to his side at him, "Oh, sorry. Try to keep up. The hall can get filled pretty fast, and they are sticklers for giving detentions for being late."

The two walked up to the boy's locker room. Timothy could see Noah take a deep breath as they walked in. He wondered what that was all about. Noah knocked on a door that read Coach Colt. It quickly sprung open. "Peters? You better not be trying to get out of gym class again."

"No Mr. Colt. I just have a new student here with me," Noah explained unenthusiastically. Timothy wondered what that was about.

Mr. Colt sized up Timothy and put out his hand, "Nice tall boy. Well, you can share a locker with Noah today. We'll figure out your locker assignment later on in the week." He went back into the office and closed the door.

Timothy was unsure what the heck he was supposed to make out of *nice tall boy*, but he would choose to let it go. He looked at Noah, who didn't say a word, and just walked down the aisle of lockers with his head down.

"Better not be looking at me change fagot," screamed a boy. A bunch of guys snickered with him. He chose to make nothing of it. This was how guys talked in a locker room setting. They finally made it back into the final row, where there were no other guys apparently.

"Do you have a gym outfit?" Noah asked him.

Timothy nodded, "Yeah. They told me I would need it right away." He put his backpack down on the bench and went in to grab it. Noah started to open his lock. Noah then took his blue jeans off. Timothy tried not to look, but he couldn't help himself. He had nice thighs and hairy legs. There was a slight bulge in his boxer briefs. Timothy quickly turned before Noah could notice what he was doing. Timothy quickly changed into his gym shorts himself. Noah then took his shirt off, revealing a slightly toned body and a slightly hairy chest with a trail around his sexy belly button. Once again, Timothy quickly turned away but was now most definitely having a boner. It was hard to hide one in gym shorts, but he casually tucked it between his legs.

Noah looked at him for a second, "Are you ok?" he wondered.

"Yeah. I'm fine, man," Timothy said. Which was the truth as his dick started to become flaccid again.

Timothy couldn't lie. There were a lot of hot guys that he had noticed so far at the school. They were just built differently; they were thicker. Not fat but just bulkier. Unlike, up east where they were much thinner. It probably had to do with dietary differences or something. Either way, it turned Timothy on. Noah, in particular, turned to look at the shirtless Timothy. He wasn't sure if he was trying to catch a glance or not, but it did last a second longer than he had looked at him. "So, I take it you don't like gym class?" Timothy asked.

"Why do you say that?" Noah asked him.

"You just don't seem thrilled to be here right now."

Noah frowned and rubbed his forehead, "No, I mean well yeah. I'm not a big fan of gym class, but it's not because of you. It's just I had a math test today I was worried about, and I thought I was going to have time to study for it during my first mod today."

Timothy frowned. So, he basically was saying that he didn't want to spend time with him. "Oh... Yeah, I get it. Um, I'm sure that I can find my way to the rest of my classes today."

"What? No! I want to help you out. Plus, Mrs. Barker seems to have put us in most of the same classes. I have no issue with helping you out. I'm just not used to being the one who gets to show people around. The counselors don't normally like it when I do that," the blond-haired boy explained.

"I can actually help you with your math. I mean not this test obviously, but I can help you in the future. That's always been my best class," Timothy admitted.

Noah smiled, "It's always been my worst class, to be honest."

"Makes sense. I mean, you are a writer," Timothy pointed out.

The Peters boy sort of blushed, "I realize I just told you about my writing, but I low-key forgot I had told you."

"So, you ready for gym?" Timothy asked him." He gestured for him to go first. He wanted to admire Noah's ass, which was beyond perfect. Timothy needed to stop falling for this guy. He didn't know if he was into guys.

* * *

Lunch on your first day at a new school was new to Timothy. He had gone to the same school district his entire life. His friends back home had been his friends for practically forever. Yet, now he was in the literal middle of nowhere, and so far, Noah was the only person he knew.

The gym class had been fine, but Timothy noticed that Noah really wasn't an athletic guy. Their next mod was actually apart, but they had the same lunch period and then the same English class at the end of the day.

The kids in his biology class were ok. They seemed nice but not overly special. It was hard to tell. It was obvious he was dressed differently than them.

Timothy looked around the room and couldn't find Noah until he noticed the blond boy sitting with a somewhat plump acid-looking red-haired girl. He walked over and sat down, "Hey Noah!"

Lily looked at him up and down. "So, you must be the new kid?" she asked. "I'm Lily."

"Nice to meet you!" Timothy said, but she didn't put out her hand to shake his back. He slowly put it back down. "So, then you and Noah are friends?"

"Yeah, definitely," Lily said. Noah looked at her a little bit more reluctantly. "So, you are from Connecticut? That's right next to New York, right? I so want to go there one day and be an actress."

This was the third girl who had mentioned wanting to be an actress to him today. He suspected that some of these girls thought that he somehow knew someone famous. He was from a small town in Connecticut, not Long Island, with connections to some trashy photographer that could secure him a daddy. Something that he never wanted for himself. "Well, I mean acting is definitely fun! Maybe Noah could write you a play to star in one day," Lily said.

Lily turned to Noah, "You write?"

Noah shrugged, "Uh yeah, sort of," he whispered.

Timothy was noticing that Lily was very much the alpha of this friendship. He wasn't so sure that he liked Lily. He suspected she was one of those people who got the understudy for the lead in the school play, but it was really just a code for the chorus where no one could hear her voice.

A boy walked up to the table and kissed Lily straight on the mouth, clearly using his tongue in a way that never should be. "Hey babe," Ned said to her as he sat down. This boy smelled like body odor and body spray. Cheap body spray that was trying to pass for *Calvin Klein*. "Who are you?" Ned asked.

"His name is Timothy. He's new," Noah said, sounding frustrated. He wasn't sure if the frustration was thrown at him or this Ned character. Looking at Lily and Ned, he could tell these two were a special kind.

"You're tall. You must play basketball," Ned said.

Timothy was starting to wonder why being tall was such a thrill to these people. Yes, he did play basketball, though. "I mean, yeah, I do."

Ned nodded, "Right on. You'll have to try out when the season starts. Gotta warn you, though, we got one hell of a powerhouse team this year. We've been practicing." He said this as if Timothy should be impressed. Timothy couldn't help but notice that Lily's hand was deep into Ned's lap. He quickly looked at Noah, who was eating a sandwich. "You have to come to the party at the barn this weekend," he explained.

"I'll have to consider it," Ned said. He looked at Noah, "Are you going?"

Noah put the sandwich down. "Uh, no, I work on the weekends and take care of my sister Kelly while my mom is at work."

Ned laughed, "Peters never hangs out with the rest of us. He has all those gay things going on for him."

"Yeah… My gay things," Noah rolled his eyes.

"You're gay, Noah?" Timothy asked, trying not to smile but also trying not to be weirded out.

"Yeah… Sorry if that was something I was supposed to tell you," he said, sounding offended that he asked.

Timothy gulped, "What? No, I don't have a problem with gay people." He looked at Ned and Lily, "Do you guys have a problem with gay people?"

Lily laughed, "I love Noah! We have been friends since forever. I know God has a place for him somewhere if he repents."

"What the fuck do I care?" Ned asked, not really looking in anyone's direction.

However, Noah looked mortified at the thought of someone asking if they were ok with him being gay. "I have to go to the bathroom," and he stood up from the table and left his tray.

Timothy had a bad feeling that he might have said something stupid.

CHAPTER THREE

NOAH

He just needed a moment alone. Noah wasn't entirely sure how he felt about this Timothy kid asking him about his sexuality. It was just weird. He had gone so long being known as the homo or queer kid and not queer in the reclaiming sense that he was put off by being asked if he was gay or not. Especially by a boy like Timothy. A guy with really nice eyes and a really hot voice.

The door opened, and Noah quickly turned and looked up to see who it was. He was sort of shocked. "Um, hey," Timothy said.

"Uh, hi," he said back.

"I didn't mean to make you uncomfortable out there," Timothy explained.

Noah shrugged, "It's nothing. I'm just used to people already knowing and either tolerating or hating me because of it."

Timothy leaned up against the sink, "Don't people just downright accept it?"

"I mean, my family does. The woman who owns the book shop is cool with it. Otherwise, not so much. Do you know Mrs. Barker? She is lowkey one of the bigger homophobes of the school," Noah explained.

"That somehow doesn't surprise me. Your friend Lily is um interesting," he explained.

The blond boy rubbed his forehead again, "Yeah… I mean, we've known each other since preschool. I've known Ned since preschool, and yes, they have always been like that. I've got good news for you. You're probably going to find your forever soulmate rather quickly around here. Probably at church," Noah explained.

The brown-haired boy laughed, "Well, I go to Temple, not church. I'm Jewish."

"Yeah, I wouldn't tell people about that around here. Regardless if you tell people, be expected to get invited to a lot of Christian youth groups," Noah explained.

"I think I'm good. Do you go to one?" Timothy asked back.

Noah nodded his head, "Sort of, I mean, I'm not anti-religion, like people for whatever reason assume. My youth group is a little more accepting, though, as opposed to the mega church that meets in the auditorium on Saturday and Sundays."

"Is that even legal for a church service to be held at a public school?" Timothy asked.

Noah shrugged, "Not entirely sure, not going to be the one to ask, though."

"So, when did you come out as gay?" Timothy wondered.

Noah felt weird talking about this with someone who was practically a stranger. Especially a really cute stranger. He was not sure if Timothy was straight or not, and he was uncertain of how to approach the subject of the brunet's sexuality. Yet, he wanted to ask. He really wanted to, but he had grown up in a community where you didn't ask those kinds of questions. He came out on his own terms. Asking someone else if they happened to be gay was not socially acceptable. At least not in Kansas, unless the person asking had a *ghost costume* at home. "A couple of years ago, I just got sick of people asking me why I didn't have a girlfriend," Noah explained. Apparently, Noah was considered attractive enough to have a girlfriend. He wasn't entirely sure what that meant. He didn't know if it meant that he was considered above average in the looks department or if he was just not ugly enough not to have a girlfriend.

"It's cool that you are able to express yourself for who you are," Timothy said with a smile on his face.

Noah looked at himself in the mirror, wearing a rather generic outfit. He owned two pairs of cowboy boots back at the house. His purple shoes were a little showier than most, but otherwise, there was nothing about him that screamed queer or queer culture. "I guess I am," he said with uncertainty.

Timothy smiled at him, "You are able to be yourself. That's more than most people."

"I'm going to be honest. I'm shocked that you didn't find a new group of friends in the last mod to have lunch with. On rare occasions, I'm made a study buddy for a new student, and they always find a new group rather quickly." Noah didn't even think it had anything to do with him being gay. He thought it had to do with the fact that he wasn't entirely over-enthusiastic about anything.

The brunet boy started to laugh, "I mean, I hope it is ok that I had lunch with you today."

"Oh yeah, no, it is perfectly fine. I just wish that Lily and Ned hadn't been there." Why did he just say that?

"Yeah, I'm not going to lie. They seem a little off, to be honest," Timothy admitted.

That was the understatement of the century. Noah was not entirely sure if he would consider Ned a friend or just Lily's boyfriend. He was not even entirely sure why he continued to spend time with Lily. When they were younger, they had been close, but by eighth grade, Noah had turned into her gay best friend even before he had come out. He was not her best friend but her gay best friend. Her parents were definitely fond of him for that reason. Yet, at the same time, they were. They clearly wanted him to be Ned. In the sense that they wanted him to be with Lily instead of Ned. Why? He assumed because they would not be having sex.

Apparently, Noah could be gay so long as it meant he would not have sex with their daughter.

"Lily means well, I guess. Ned is… I don't know. They will probably get married before twenty-one. Just like my brother and his girlfriend will," Noah explained.

"Oh, your brother is married?" Timothy asked.

Noah sighed, "No... Not yet, but I'm going to be an uncle in a couple of months."

The East Coast boy nodded, "Oh... That's cool."

"That's this town for you..." He was sure that in a month, Timothy would have some girl all over him day and night, and they would be on the verge of marriage by the end of their senior year and probably expecting a child of their own. He was sure that in Connecticut, that would be horrible to think. Here, it was also horrible to think, but why prolong the inevitable to your thirties when you can just get pregnant outside of high school? That's what happened to Brick. Brick was actually a pretty smart guy, which was the sad thing.

"I mean, being an uncle will probably be fun. Who doesn't enjoy a good baby?" Timothy pointed out with a smile.

In reality, he had a good point. Everyone loved babies. He just knew that between Brick and his mother, he would most definitely be helping raise the child. His girlfriend's parents pretty much blamed the entire family for all of this. Brick mentioned that apparently, his girlfriend had been out of birth control and neglected to mention it. Noah thought that was deceitful, but it wasn't his place to point that out.

The bell rang. Lunch was wrapping up soon. "So, um, last class for the day. Do you think you can show me where it is?" Timothy asked with an adorable smile.

Noah nodded, "Yeah, no problem."

* * *

The last class for the day was relatively uneventful. The entire day had been rather uneventful in Noah's mind, aside from Timothy. Timothy, the tall brunet boy with a sexy deep voice. Noah needed to focus. He had about two hundred books to get shelved before the end of his shift, which was not so bad.

The owner of the bookstore was a woman named Sasha in her late 20's. Total hipster type. Apparently, when she first bought the place from a sweet older couple, she wanted to revitalize it completely. It was going to be nothing but bestsellers, classics, and indie authors. Then she realized just how little people seemed to buy books unless they were romance or western novels. Crime was big as well, but more for the online store. She ended up having to bite the bullet and keep the two sections. Noah often caught Sasha reading the Western novels. Sometimes she would be laughing, and sometimes she would be genuinely into them.

Sasha was a cool boss. If Noah was honest, he was probably more friends with her than he was Lily. They never talked about sexuality. They talked about life. Which, on occasion, involved crushes they had on men or different aspects of queer culture as Sasha herself was bisexual. Though when they talked about different men they had crushes on, Noah often had to talk about different actors he found attractive. He wasn't all that attracted to the straight or closeted men that were around him.

He would often ask why Sasha didn't leave Kansas. She would just say that she was a big fish in a small pond here. Anywhere else, she would be a small fish in a big pond. That was how smart she was. Sasha knew that she was special and different here, but she would be no one in some big city. Noah realized the sentiment was smart, but it didn't change his own views. Noah wanted out of this state by the time he graduated. Just two years to go. He could get through his junior and senior years. He could do it. Noah just had to keep telling himself that he would make it through.

"Noah, sweetie, I have to go pick up a shipment at the post office in the next city over. I'll be back in about an hour," Sasha explained as she grabbed her sweater and keys.

The blond boy nodded. He was used to her leaving for an hour or so every once in a while at this point. Very rarely did they ever need two people there. The online business essentially paid for the rent. Sasha's family came from a little bit of money. That was how she afforded the lifestyle, which wasn't that hard in Kansas.

The door opened again. Noah honestly thought it was going to be Sasha telling him that she forgot something. Instead, it was him… "Timothy? What are you doing here?"

He had the biggest smile on his face, "Um, I just thought I'd stop in and say hi. I hope that's cool." It had only been a few hours since school had gotten out. Lily had never once come to visit him at work.

"Yeah, totally. I just never expected anyone to come here. I mean, I rarely ever see people from school, and if I do, it is usually just someone really into science fiction or something that I don't even know the name of," Noah admitted while almost rambling.

Timothy nodded, "Yeah, I love to read, and our internet hasn't been connected yet. I just wanted to pick up a few extra books to pass the time." He went over to a shelf. "It's kind of weird not having homework, though," he admitted.

"Well, they could either afford to buy textbooks for all the students to bring home, or they could afford upgrades to the football field," Noah explained.

"I have to admit that the way the teachers teach is scaring me. One of my teachers just played videos during the entire class," he said.

The blond boy nodded, "Yeah… That's how this goes, pretty much. There are some teachers who want to teach. Then there are those who gave up a long time ago. You probably notice a lot of the teachers are from Texas, Oklahoma, or other places entirely. That should tell you something."

Timothy looked around the room, "This is low-key a nice little shop."

"Yeah, when Sasha took over, she really did try and revitalize the space. It used to look more used bookstore like." They had actually spent the entire week painting the store, setting up new shelves, and revitalizing old shelves that were still practical. It was such a cool shop with all the changes. "I don't think she will keep it for much longer, though," Noah explained.

"Why?" Timothy asked.

"Eh, not really a money maker. Her parents help foot the bill. She makes more from an online standpoint. I think she is low-key, keeping it open to keep me employed." Noah really did think this was the case. Sasha often joked about opening a nightclub when he graduated high school. He didn't think much of it at first, but he saw the computer browsing history enough times to know it was probably true. He was grateful for Sasha. He really was.

The door opened again. He assumed that Sasha really was back this time, but instead, it was Brick, "Hey Noah… I need a few books for Amber's classes. They are too expensive at the chain store. I need the nicest copies you have."

Noah coughed, "Um, Brick, this is Timothy. Timothy, this is Brick, my older brother," he looked at Brick. "Timothy is new at school, and we were just talking."

Brick looked at the boy and smiled. He put his hand out, "Oh, hey! Nice to meet you." The two boys shook hands. Brick looked back at Noah and gave him this look of approval. Noah knew what that look was. He used to give him that look back when he was in middle school and thought he was into girls. Brick used to give him a look of approval. Noah's stomach started to jump. He would have to explain later on that Timothy wasn't that kind of a friend; at least he didn't think he was.

Brick handed Noah the list, "Amber is freaking out."

The younger brother read the list from his older brother, "Oh, for crying out loud, Brick." Half these books were brand new releases. "We don't have any of these. Well, actually, no, I have one of these." He walked back to the section where it would be. Noah was sure that he was quick to get it, considering that he really didn't want Brick or Timothy talking with one another. "Here you go; Your copy of *To Kill a Mockingbird*."

"Thanks, man. I guess I'll have to get the rest somewhere else," his older brother explained.

Timothy smiled, "Oh, I love that book. We read it in ninth grade. I'm shocked they are having your girlfriend read it on a college level."

Noah grunted, "Yeah, well, there were too many students offended by it. It was mostly the tone-deaf interpretation being presented. Plus, they wouldn't even let people read the entire book. Just the parts that they felt were important for test questions." Noah still remembered that town hall meeting. This town was doomed.

The new boy dropped the smile that he always seemed to have on his face and just nodded, "How interesting…" If Noah were reading between the lines, he could tell that it disgusted him just as much.

Brick coughed, "I'll see you at home, Bro. Or well, maybe I won't. I'm working a double tonight. Later!" He winked and ran out.

"Your brother seems nice. You look like a slightly more muscular version of him," Timothy said, kind of flirty, but it felt like a weird thing to be flirty about. At least Noah thought so.

"Yeah. He used to be more muscular than I was, but over the last few months, he has been stressed out with the baby on the way," Noah explained. He wished that Brick had just gone to school as he had intended. Noah looked outside and noticed a bike. "Did you ride your bike here?"

Timothy nodded, "Yeah. My car didn't make the drive over from the East Coast. It was a clunker. I'll get a new one soon."

Did Noah dare ask him this...? He was going to take the shot, "Do you want a ride to school tomorrow morning?" There he made the next gesture into hanging out more with this guy, this really hot guy.

"Oh, I don't want to be a burden," Timothy explained.

Damn it. Thought Noah, "No! It's no issue at all. I can get you. I have to take my sister to school is the only issue."

Timothy pondered for a moment; it seemed, "Ok, yeah. Um, here," he wrote something down on a flier that was on the front desk. "This is my number. Just text me later on, and I'll text my address and when I should be up to meet you. Thanks, man!"

Noah was trying to avoid having the world's biggest smile on his face, but he couldn't help it. He knew that they would be spending the day at school tomorrow to some degree, but the extra few minutes in the morning just felt epic. That was the word he was using in his mind. Epic.

CHAPTER FOUR

TIMOTHY

The more that Noah described Kansas, the less he was sure about this place. Yet the more he talked with Noah, the more he liked spending time with him. He was adorable in the most farm boy way possible. Timothy wasn't entirely sure if that was considered offensive or not, but he felt like it was suitable.

He walked his bike into his new garage and parked it along the side. He then went in from the garage door into the house. Timothy walked into the kitchen, where his mother was making dinner. "Hey," he said.

"Where did you run off to?" Ana asked. Ana was a typical Jewish mother. Overly protective, but at the same time, she gave Timothy a lot of space, or at least that is what she claimed. He supposed that in comparison to a lot of his Jewish friends back home, she did.

"I just went exploring a little on my bike. You realize you have sent me to a school that doesn't give homework, right?" he pointed out.

Ana put her arms on her hips, "Well when I go and talk with your teachers, they will have homework for you." This was typical of his mother. She wasn't going to let him get away without studying, which is something she always did.

Timothy looked around the room. It was slightly larger than their old house. It wasn't a terrible house, definitely on the nicer side of town. Yet, it was still pretty meh. "When is dad supposed to be home?" Timothy asked.

"Oh, I'm sure on the later side. He still is adjusting to working and what have you. We just have to give it a few weeks, and things will be back to normal," Ana explained to her son.

Would things ever be back to normal? Connecticut was so different from Kansas. Noah had essentially made Kansas seem like hell on earth in a day. "I suppose we will adjust."

Ana smiled, "So, then did you make any friends at school today?"

It felt weird to hear her ask that. That sounded like something that a parent would ask a child in a bad sitcom or something. "I mean, there are some nice kids in a few of my classes. There is this one guy who will be picking me up tomorrow morning," Timothy explained.

His mother continued to smile, "See, you thought that it would take you forever to make a friend!" Ana explained.

Was Noah a friend? I mean yeah, he guessed. There was just something about Noah that seemed very weird but in a good way. "I'm going to go Facetime with the guys back home," Timothy explained before he pondered the subject of Noah anymore.

* * *

Timothy's new room was slightly smaller than the one he had back home. The closet was much larger, so that was a plus considering how much clothes he acquired over the years. He never really thought about how many outfits he had until he had to not only pack everything up but then unpack it.

The curly-haired boy sat down at his desk and opened his laptop. It only took a minute for the video call to start up with his two best friends from back home, Collin and Philip. They were all on the same basketball teams from the time they were five years old. Timothy still intended to go to college with them. The world could separate the three friends apart, but it wouldn't stop their friendship.

"What up, man!" Collin screamed into his microphone.

"A whole lot of nothing," Timothy explained to the redhead. "There is like nothing to do around here."

Philip put on his very familiar, told you so smile, "Yeah, my aunt lives in Kansas. We kind of force her to come to visit us instead of the other way around. It's just so boring down there. Good golf game though, I guess, but it is pretty flat."

Timothy shrugged, "I haven't gotten to explore very much as of yet. Possibly this weekend. I don't know. Not a whole lot of people to go exploring with," Timothy explained as he once again thought about Noah. He needed to stop thinking about Noah.

"So, any potential new girlfriends out there?" Phillip obnoxiously asked.

"Eh, not that I can see... It seems like everyone is paired up rather well down here already," Timothy explained.

"Tara is still taking it pretty hard," Collin frowned.

Tara Milton. Timothy and Tara had been together since fifth grade off and on, but more times on. He loved her, but he loved the concept more than the execution of her. In many ways, she was the fourth member of the group of friends. She wasn't really a traditional girlfriend. Yet, she was. "Yeah, I've texted a little bit with her. I don't know...."

Collin frowned in sympathy, "So, you still plan on coming up for Thanksgiving and Christmas, right?"

Timothy smiled, "Yeah, that is the plan as of now. We'll hang out every free minute that we get away from our families. It's so weird to be away from you guys." It really was. If he wasn't at home, he was with either Collin or Phillip, or both, or Tara. That was their friendship. Timothy was still angry at his parents for breaking apart their friendship. He knew that they were just trying to do what was best for the family but still. There are parts of his life that he was starting to realize about himself, and he would have rather explored them with Phillip and Collin and even Tara around.

Timothy was honestly unsure if he was gay or bi, or whatever. Yet, he couldn't deny the fact that he had some attraction to Noah. The same went for a few guys back home. Then there was the fact that he spent hours looking at pictures of famous men like Tom Holland or Harry Styles. Yet, he didn't find that same attraction to men like Collin or Phillip. Could it be because he grew up with them and thought of them as family? He had to think that was the reason.

Then there was Tara. She was beautiful, but whenever they started to get to the sex stages, they always stopped themselves. Or well, he stopped himself. Tara was clearly ready to lose her virginity. Timothy was also ready to lose his virginity. He just knew that deep down, it wasn't meant to be with her. Was it meant to be with a guy, though? He never looked at gay porn. He really didn't look at porn at all.

"You missed a killer game after school today," Collin pointed out.

"Oh yeah? Who beat who?" Timothy asked, genuinely intrigued.

Phillip laughed, "Uh, no one dude. We both suck at ball. You were the only one with talent."

"Damn right, I am," Timothy said with a little bit of confidence. Something he had lacked the last few days.

CHAPTER FIVE

NOAH

"So, how was your day?" Cheryl asked her middle child as she put down a plate in front of him at the kitchen table.

Noah shrugged, "Normal." He lied, sort of. Aside from Timothy, though, nothing was out of the ordinary.

Kelly gave him a dirty look, "I had to walk home again because of you."

"That's nice," he told his younger sister. What did he care if she had to walk home? He had to walk home for years.

Brick sat down, "I think Noah found himself a guy." He put out his hand to give a high five. Noah gave him a weird look.

"That's just some new kid. I don't think he is gay."

"Well, how will you know until you ask honey?" Cheryl asked as she put a large helping of mashed potatoes on her plate.

All three of her children looked at her, "That's not exactly how it works in this town, mom. I mean, unless you want to come and pick me up at the hospital."

Cheryl rolled her eyes, "Noah, you don't give the people of this town enough credit. Aside from the people who shop at Target, now those people would shoot you."

He sometimes wasn't sure if his mother was trying to be funny and caring or if she just wasn't entirely sure how to handle the narrative of having an LGBTQ teenage son. It wasn't that Cheryl wasn't supportive when he came out. The entire family, aside from a few rogue cousins, were. It was the fact that it was clear that unless they were deeply in the closet, no one in the Peters family was ever LGBTQ. Then Noah came along and changed that up for the history books of their easily forgettable family. If anything, his being gay gave them something to discuss. Generations of boring people finally got something—a gay guy.

"Oh, come on, Noah, you clearly had a thing for him," Brick annoyingly pointed out. Why did his brother have to be supportive of him? Then again, he supposed that this would be how he would be, had it been a girl as well. "You should totally hang out with him a little more."

"I am driving him to school tomorrow morning," Noah blurted out. Why did he say that? He figured that Kelly would have said something tomorrow regardless, though.

Kelly gave this evil smile, "Well, then I will get to meet him and find out if he is gay. I have incredible gaydar."

Noah looked at his younger sister, "That's not offensive at all. How can you tell if someone is gay or not by just looking at them?" Did people look at him and think that? He had to be honest and think probably. However, heteronomy made him hope otherwise.

Brick looked at his phone, "I just got a text at work. They need me to cover a shift."

"Oh, come on, Brick, just stay home for the night," Noah sighed. He wanted to play video games together. As of late, he only ever saw Brick in passing.

"Nah, I've got to save every dollar I can for the baby. I'll be home late." He sat up from the kitchen table and kissed Cheryl goodbye. He walked out the backdoor.

Their mother sighed, "I'm getting tired of him putting all the effort in the world towards Amber."

Thank goodness someone else said it, "Do we actually think they are going to get married?" Noah asked?

"I don't know... I'll support them if they get married, and obviously, I'll love my grandchild, but Amber better step up and do something with that damn degree she is getting right now. Why my son has to work two jobs while she gets babied over having a baby is beyond me," Cheryl stated.

This was really the first time that his mom had ever said anything nasty about Amber since they found out she was pregnant. Cheryl was never a big fan of her when Brick and Amber were in high school dating. Noah had to admit he wasn't a big fan of her himself. Her family always acted like they were better than everyone around them. It just was bullshit. Their home might have been slightly larger, but they lived in the middle of nowhere, Kansas as well.

* * *

"Finally done," Noah said out loud as he finished studying for the night. He looked at the essay he wrote for his college entry. He was still a year away from having to worry about this stuff. Yet, his teachers had no common sense, so here he was.

Aside from the summer, Noah knew deep down that there was no way he would be living in Kansas after graduation from high school. He was determined to move far away and start a new life where he could be himself.

He never touched a dime of the money he got from working besides his car insurance and gas money. He saved the birthday and Christmas money he got from family. Noah was determined to move out west come fall of his Freshman year of college, even if he was going to a community college or something.

He thought about the day in general. It was definitely a weird day, at least for him. He wasn't used to having conversations with people that went deeper on his end. Timothy was different on so many levels than the men and people in general that had been around him. He didn't think that Timothy was gay. He wasn't sure. Noah had no idea how to tell if he was gay, and he was nervous about approaching the subject. If he asked, then Timothy was going to think that he was asking him out essentially. If Timothy was straight, then he might blow up a potential friend, and Noah only had a few, to begin with. The blonde boy had to wonder, was it necessary to be in a relationship that could turn out messy? Having a friend is more important. He would find love one day. He was still a teenager, after all.

Noah started to undress for bed. He made sure to put on his facial lotion right before getting into bed. He didn't need to break out the next morning and have Timothy get turned off. The blond boy slipped under the covers of his bed but couldn't sleep. He kept saying Timothy's name over and over in his head. Timothy Powel, Timothy Powel, Timothy Powel. He needed a middle name so he could have some variation. Timothy Peters..., Noah Powel ..., his curly hair ..., his pale but sexy skin with stubble all over. Noah was starting to get hard and needed relief. Before he could get on to touching himself, his phone pinged. It was a notification that Timothy was now following him on Facebook and Insta. He quickly friended and followed back. He scrolled down his Insta feed and saw many pictures, some of which were clearly with his family and others with friends. He noticed a few pictures with a girl.... A girl! He clicked on them, and there were no indications that she was a girlfriend, a friend, or a cousin, but she was in a lot of these pics.

As he tried to move past this mystery girl, a message popped up on his messenger. It was Timothy requesting to facetime. Noah was shirtless in bed. He didn't have time to put one on, though, and he wanted... No... needed to take this call. He hit accept, and it connected him to Timothy, who was also in bed but had a shirt on. "Hey," Noah said, very awkwardly.

"Hey!" Timothy said with a smile on his face a little excitedly. He looked at Noah for a second and turned red, "Sorry, didn't know if you were sleeping or not."

"Oh, no! I mean, I was about to get to bed but also kinda hard... hard to get to bed." Fuck. Did he seriously just say that?

The curly-haired boy nodded, "Yeah, my sleep schedule is a little fucked up. I never sleep that much except on like Sunday. It doesn't help that it is technically an hour earlier here."

He completely forgot that Kansas was in a different time zone. "Oh yeah, that must be rough..." Noah's hardon was getting harder and harder as he looked at Timothy. He knew that he was testing the waters, but he sat up in bed, revealing his toned chest. He pretended to yawn a little bit as he showed off. His nipples were definitely hard.

"Do you work out a lot?" Timothy asked.

"Uh... I try. I mean, we only have the one gym in town. I try to do pushups and stuff." He felt like that was asked in a flirty way. It wasn't like Noah had a very muscular body.

The curly-haired boy smiled, "Very nice. We should work out sometime."

Noah smiled this time, "Yeah, man, I'd like that."

Timothy stayed silent for a moment. "Do you want to see my pecs? I need to work on them, but I need an opinion on if I have them or not," he laughed very awkwardly.

Oh, fuck... "Yeah... Sure." Noah hardly got out. Noah didn't want to assume, but it definitely felt like Timothy was flirting with him. Why would another guy ask to take his shirt off for him?

His new friend quickly slipped off his shirt. Damn was all Noah could think. It wasn't even the first time that he saw Timothy shirtless but still. "What do you think?" he asked.

"Fuck....," Noah turned bright red as he realized that he said that out loud. "I mean, um....," Noah couldn't deny it, "Look, Timothy, you look great."

"Thanks," Timothy responded sheepishly. Noah thought his response was hot.

"You seem to have a great body," Noah admitted.

Timothy smiled but was also silent for a minute, "Do... Do you want to see more?" he asked.

Noah turned completely white, "Um... What do you mean?"

The curly-haired boy looked at him very shyly. He lifted his camera up and pulled the covers down from around his torso. He was wearing briefs with a big hardon himself. Noah looked in complete shock for a second, "Can I see it?"

Timothy nodded. He pulled down his shorts with his one hand. Out popped his very thick cut member. He quickly returned to his face. "Do you like it?" Timothy asked.

Noah nodded, biting on his lip. "I was thinking about you right before you called," he admitted.

"I've been thinking about you non-stop since I got home," Timothy told him.

This went from being the most typical day of Noah's life to one of the best, "You have beautiful eyes."

His new friend hesitated to respond, "You do too."

"I wish you were here right now," Noah admitted.

"I wish I was there too," Timothy said, very flirty.

CHAPTER SIX

TIMOTHY

He couldn't believe what he had done the night before. That was the first time that he had ever sexted with someone. Timothy had never even done that with Tara. Normally, he would never. Yet…, Noah. There was just something about him that made him want to do that with him.

Timothy had to admit that he had never really known any openly gay guys back home. That was technically his first time experimenting with anyone. The conversation sort of went back to the two of them flirting after he showed off to Noah. He had been hoping that Noah would share the rest of his body with him, but he didn't want to ask out of making him feel pressured. He had no idea how this whole gay thing worked and what was considered appropriate and what wasn't. All he knew was that Noah quite possibly was hornier than he had been when he had called him. Timothy wasn't going to lie. He wanted Noah badly now.

The curly-haired boy hardly slept after their call ended last night. Noah remembered to remind him that he would be picking him up this morning. He needed to wear something that Noah would find sexy. Did people use the word sexy anymore? Timothy had no idea. He put on a fitted black and white flannel shirt, with a pair of brown corduroy skinny jeans that were extra tight. He also made sure to wear his tightest pair of CK briefs that happened to be purple. He wore long black dress socks that he had pulled up on his legs. He made sure to wear a pair of clean Nikes. Timothy spent an extra ten minutes doing his hair and brushed his teeth four times over. He was abusing breath mints. "Oh, get it together, Powel. We are going to school for the day, not hooking up." Though, he wished they were going to. Timothy was so ready to lose his virginity, and, at this moment, he wanted it to be with his new friend Noah.

His phone went off. It was Noah saying that he was in his driveway, and his sister was with him. He took that reminder as a double reminder to play it cool.

* * *

Timothy walked outside, carrying his backpack around his shoulder, very nervous. This was so weird and awkward. He wanted to retort back to his bedroom and hide. All his confidence was gone seeing Noah in person again. It had only been like twenty-something hours since he had met Noah, and he had already seen him naked from afar, mind you, and was ready to see him naked in person. He wanted to touch and be touched by Noah so badly. He should have waited a few more days so this could happen on the weekend and they would have more alone time.

He got into the car and smiled, "Hey, Noah! Thanks for picking me up." He automatically reached out into the backseat and went to shake his younger sister's hand, "Hi, I'm Timothy."

His younger sister shook his hand back, "I'm Kelly... So, you're Timothy?" She asked, giving this weird look to Noah and not him.

Timothy wondered if Noah had mentioned anything to his sister. It would have been weird if he did, considering she looked like she was thirteen, but who knew. It wasn't like he had a sibling to discuss love and sex with. Though, would he actually be willing to do so with a sibling? Probably not.

Noah said nothing as they drove down the street. Kelly had her headphones on, while Noah leaned his arm on the armrest. Timothy took this as a quick gesture but got nervous with his sister in the backseat. All he ended up doing was brushing his hand against Noah's but quickly moving it. Noah clearly got uncomfortable and put both hands back on the wheel. They made it to Kelly's school and dropped her off. She moaned when he told her she was walking home again.

The two boys were left alone again. They both seemed to sigh at the same time. Noah, all of a sudden, parked the car in the parking lot. He turned to Timothy, "I need to know something before I spend the rest of the day agonizing over it... Are you gay?"

Timothy gulped. Was he? "I... I don't know," he buried his head in his lap. Noah put his hand on his back, "I've had the same girlfriend since like forever, but we broke up when I moved away. It's just over the last few years I've started to notice guys," Timothy explained.

"So, then you are bi? Pan? Curious?" Noah asked, very panicky.

The curly-haired boy picked his head back up, "Look, man, I don't know what I am. I just know that I think you have beautiful eyes, and you turn me on." He started to think. Did he experiment with Noah because he happened to be gay? No. He thought he was cute the moment he laid eyes on him. He had no idea that he was gay at that point.

Noah sighed again, "I think you are really cute too. It's just, well, I've never had a boyfriend before. Just a series of supposedly straight men who get horny and want to do things but then never look at me again. I don't want to do that anymore."

"What? No! I don't want to do anything you aren't ready for. I don't even know what I'm ready for. I'm a virgin," the boy whispered.

"Oh... Really?" Noah asked.

Timothy nodded his head, "We don't have to have sex. We don't have to do anything sexual if you don't want to. I can live with just being your friend if that is all you want." The Powel boy lied. He wanted more, but he had no idea what more was.

"Can I kiss you?" Noah asked.

Timothy didn't even respond; he just leaned in and started kissing Noah. It was weird. Noah had a little bit of stubble around his lips, which Timothy could feel. He also smelled like a guy, which was hot. He quickly started to wrap his arms around Noah but lowering his hand to the blond boy's thigh. They stopped. "Sorry..." Noah grabbed Timothy's hand and put it back on his inner thigh. Timothy went in more until he was directly touching Noah's groin. He was clearly hard, and he had something big packed away down there.

The two boys looked at one another. Timothy went back and forth between looking at Noah's crotch and looking at his eyes. Noah sort of nodded as if he knew exactly what he was thinking. The brunet boy unzipped Noah's jeans and reached inside to his briefs. Noah started to help him out and took out his large uncut member. Timothy was hesitant but touched the tip. He stroked it a few times before he stopped, "I um… I don't want to get caught."

Noah was breathing heavily. He nodded, though, after he seemed to come back to reality. He put his dick away and took a minute to rearrange himself. "That was the first time a guy has ever touched me," the blond boy admitted.

"I thought you said you had done stuff with guys before?" Timothy asked.

"Yeah… I've done stuff to guys. They never want to reciprocate," Noah frowned.

This was honestly in one of the top five moments in his life, "I'd like to do more with you." He wanted to be with Noah, "I'd like to do more than just that, though."

"Yeah… Definitely more than just hand jobs," Noah smiled eagerly.

The curly-haired boy shook his head. "No… I mean, I'd like to hang out like on a date or something," he said nervously.

"I'd love that!" Noah said, blushing. He looked down at the clock. "Fuck, we are late! That homophobic councilor is going to let me have it."

He thought for a second, "Do you want to just skip the day?"

It took a moment for Noah to respond, "Do you want to go to the mall or something?"

That sounded much better than school. "Yeah. We just need to figure out how to call off," Timothy stated.

"They don't call off here. You just send in a note with you the next day. Kind of stupid, but that is how they do it," Noah explained.

Perfect Timothy thought. "Great. Let's go hang out at the mall."

"This doesn't count as a date, though. I want to take you somewhere nice," Noah explained.

"What if I wanted to take you somewhere nice?" Timothy asked back.

His new friend shook his head, "Nope. You asked me out, so I get to be the one to treat you like a king."

Treat him like a king? Timothy felt special in a way that he never had before. "Ok. But like that doesn't make me the girl, right?"

Noah looked at him in confusion, "Timothy, neither one of us has to take on a gender role, regardless of who does what to the other, if it even gets that far. We are both men."

"Sorry, that sounded so crude now that I've said it," Timothy felt like a jerk. It was almost like he was insinuating that he wanted Noah to be the female in a relationship like that somehow lessened one or the other.

"No… You are new to this. Just promise me if it turns out you aren't into this at all that you will let me down easily," Noah frowned.

While this was a new road for Timothy to walk down, he had no intention of hurting the beautiful blond-haired boy ever, "I promise, dude." Was dude appropriate to call his potential boyfriend? Were they boyfriends? It was way too soon to label this, and he wasn't going to be the one to ask that question right now.

Noah sighed. He went in and kissed Timothy himself. He stopped himself after a minute or so, "I just needed to make sure that this happened. Fuck, you are so beautiful, and you like me?"

Was it too early to admit that yeah, he did like him? "I mean, I want to get to know you in every single sense of the word for sure," said Noah.

CHAPTER SEVEN

NOAH

This finally happened. A guy kissed him. A boy with beautiful eyes and full lips kissed him and kissed him first. Timothy also touched him in a way that he had only ever dreamed about. It felt amazing....Timothy was amazing. However, he knew they needed to slow down. The blond boy had no intention of losing this boy because all they had in common was sex. Even if he really wanted to do it with him every chance, they got.

It took about twenty minutes to get to the mall. Noah realized rather quickly that there wasn't much to even do at the mall. There were no exciting clothing stores and no music shops. This was going to be a boring afternoon. He just had a bad feeling.

Timothy sort of shuffled around in his seat, "So, um, your sister seems cool," he said randomly.

Clearly, he was trying to change the subject to avoid making things weird. He just felt like changing the subject from sex to his sister was bizarre. "Oh, um, she is actually a pretty big brat. My older brother Brick is pretty cool, though," said Noah.

"Oh yeah, totally, he seemed great! I wish I had brothers or sisters. I have some cousins, but it wasn't like we hung out all day every day," Timothy explained.

Noah snorted, "I wouldn't say I have ever spent all day and every day with either of my siblings. I mean, Brick and I get along for the most part now. However, when we were younger, we always fought. I guess that is just how brothers are."

Timothy looked out the window, "There are a lot of fields out there."

Oh, yes, there were. "You know I've lived here my entire life, and I still have no idea who even owns those fields. They could be all owned by the same person or the government for all I know," Noah admitted.

"Oh, look horses! I used to go riding when I was a little younger," the curly-haired boy gave Noah the biggest of smiles.

If he were honest, he had to admit that horses kind of freaked him out. "We could go riding sometime if you wanted!" Noah suggested.

The curly-haired boy smiled again, "Oh yeah, that would be freaking awesome!"

His smile was infectious. Noah wanted to play with his hair as well. Not even in a sexual way. He just loved Timothy's curly hair.

They made their way to the mall parking lot when Noah suddenly had a come to Jesus moment, "We can't hold hands or be handsy with one another in there." He looked right into Timothy's eyes.

"What do you mean?" Timothy asked.

"Look… I'm not saying that everyone in Kansas is homophobic, but the amount of *I don't have an issue with queer people* starts to change when they actually see two guys or girls or whatever walking around in the wild." Noah knew from experience. Wearing a rainbow bracelet during pride month was not one of his more brilliant ideas. "It's not that I don't want to or that I'm even scared. It's just the way things are."

Timothy nodded, "No, I get it. I mean, it is probably best we stay low key. We don't want to get caught."

It was so obvious Timothy was sad that they wouldn't be holding hands. It almost broke Noah's heart. If he was honest, it did. It totally did…, "We could go to the park later on, though, and be a little more open. We just can't go right now, considering that the police tend to hang out there." This made the brown-haired boy smile.

This was clearly new territory for both boys. It was a thrill for Noah at least to be hanging out with Timothy. He knew that this wasn't a date, but it was at current the closest thing he had ever had to a date.

* * *

As expected, the mall was pretty dead aside from older people doing laps and mother's wandering around with young children. It was such a boring mall, and the more Noah looked at it, realized that it was also kind of filthy.

"Do you want a pretzel?" Timothy asked.

Noah took out his wallet. Timothy gave him a dirty look, "I got this, don't worry."

Timothy rolled his eyes, "I've got it." He took out his own wallet and walked over to the pretzel shop. He returned a minute or so later with two large pretzels. "Here!" the beautiful, smiling boy said.

This was going to be weird. Timothy was used to being the boyfriend of a girlfriend. Noah had never been a boyfriend to anyone. This was all new to both of them. It was hard not to fall for this guy, though. He was so adorable, and the super-deep voice made him even hotter.

The two boys continued to walk throughout the mall. It only took about twenty minutes for them to both realize that they had literally nothing to do.

"Should we try going somewhere else?" Noah wondered.

Timothy shrugged, "I mean, I don't mind. I just don't have any idea where we could go, obviously."

Noah thought about it for a minute. He realized that it would be a risk but then decided it would be better than nothing. "Do you want to just go back to my place?"

The brown-haired boy had a smile on his face, "Yeah, that be cool. Do we need to worry about your family though being around?"

"Not right now. My mom works until like nine tonight, and Brick is probably out for the rest of the day as well. We just have to be out of there before Kelly gets home," Noah explained. Timothy was back to smiling in a way that clearly meant something that Noah wasn't intending on. "I just want to hang out." He obviously wanted to do more, but he also didn't want to rush things.

"Oh no, I get it," Timothy said with a slight frown but trying to smile.

This boy was going to be a handful, and Noah was ready for every single second of it a thousand times over.

* * *

Upon arriving on his block, he realized that Timothy lived in one of the nicer parts of the town. Noah hardly lived in a dump, but it felt lived in by comparison. The front lawn was in desperate need of a mow. The mailbox was rusting. One of the numbers on his address had fallen off, and the shadow was all that was remaining. In comparison to the other homes on the block, it looked fine, in any case. Timothy didn't seem bothered by it, but that didn't change Noah being nervous about it.

They each got out of the car. The blond made sure that he parked in the garage just in case a random neighbor saw them. The two walked into the kitchen from the side door. It seemed that people only really ever looked at their homes when outsiders entered them. It definitely could have been cleaner, but it was lived in.

Timothy instantly noticed a photo of him from a few years back on the fridge. "You look so adorable here." Noah tried to cover it from further inspection, but Timothy stopped him, "Oh, don't worry, dude... Really, you look adorable here. You look even more adorable now in person."

Noah wanted to take him right then and there but knew that wasn't going to happen. Instead, they walked into the living room. There were old magazines layered on the coffee table along with the mail. The couch looked lived on, but Noah knew that he had to offer the boy somewhere to sit, so he did, and Noah sat next to him. They instantly sunk into one another. They looked into one another's eyes. Noah couldn't help it, he kissed the boy again and again and again.

"Your lips are perfect," Timothy said.

His lips were perfect too. He had beautiful dimples and amazing eyes. Everything about him was just amazing. "Thanks," was all that Noah could say.

"So, what do you watch on TV?" Timothy asked.

"Uh... I don't know, just whatever is on."

The brown-haired boy nodded, "Do you watch that drag queen show?" he sort of whispered as if someone would overhear.

"I'm not really into drag queens," Noah explained. He looked at Timothy, who looked a little saddened by this. "It's cool if you do, though. I'm sure we could find a bar to sneak in and see one or something if you wanted."

Timothy laughed, "Oh, I've only ever seen a few clips of it. They look cool, but no, I don't watch it or anything. I was just wondering," Timothy said.

Noah felt his phone vibrate and looked down. It was Lily asking where he was. He considered texting her back but chose not to.

"Who is it?" Timothy asked him, "You don't have to answer. Sorry, didn't mean to be intrusive."

"What? Oh, no, it's fine. It was just my friend Lily," Noah explained.

The Brown-haired boy nodded, "Yeah, she really doesn't seem like a great friend, to be completely honest."

He knew this, and his family knew this. Lily just happened to be the only person at that godawful school that would willingly associate themselves with him regularly. "I mean, she is what she is. I doubt I'll stay in touch with her after high school."

"You don't have to stay friends with someone that is kind of, well... like her," Timothy pointed out.

This boy had a lot to learn, "Eh... Lily is tame in comparison to some of the people at that school." He couldn't help but think of some of the people he had been going to school with since elementary school, which was most of his class if he was honest. "We could hang out with her sometime. I'm sure you won't completely hate her," Noah said.

Timothy put a small smile on his face. It was obvious that this wasn't something he was going to be looking forward to.

CHAPTER EIGHT

TIMOTHY

Today was one of the best days of his life. It was beyond boring in explanation and yet such a rush. Timothy would never have skipped school back in Connecticut, even with his group of friends. The curly-haired boy had to admit that he wasn't very fond of Lily or her boyfriend and wasn't looking forward to having to spend time with her. There was just something off about both of them. There was something off about a lot of people in the town. They were very *Stepford*.

Timothy walked into his bedroom and sat down on his bed. He looked around the room. He had sat on this bed for a good ten years of his life and used the dressers for almost as long. The desk where his computer sat was about four years old, along with the desktop that sat on it. He tried to place the furniture in the same place they were in his old bedroom. There were a few differences in things. His window was no longer in the middle, but now off to the side closest where he woke up in the morning, which felt off. He also had his own bathroom in this house, which meant that his dresser was centered where his bed was. Something about everything going on made him realize that change had happened. He obviously wasn't in Connecticut anymore.

The teenage boy stood up from his bed and pushed it aside. He moved his desk to where it currently stood and pushed the bed next to where the dresser was. That way, he didn't wake up to the sun blaring even with the blinds supposedly covering it. He then went into his closet. It was a small walk in. He looked around at his clothes. Were they really him anymore? He heard footsteps and turned around. His mother was standing there, confused.

"Are you ok?" she asked him.

He laughed, "Yeah, you scared me for a second."

She turned and looked at his room, "Reorganizing already?"

Timothy shrugged, "I just felt like I needed change. We aren't home anymore.

His mother frowned, "This is your home, though."

"Yeah, I know it is my home now, which is what I mean. I felt like I was holding on to a person that I wasn't anymore," Timothy sighed. His mother didn't seem to get what he meant, and he felt bad.

Ana put her hand on his shoulder, "Oh, honey, I don't think we ever really asked you how the move was affecting you." She walked out of the closet and sat on his bed, which was now further from the closet.

There was a distance between them. Timothy walked out of the closet himself, "I'm honestly fine with it. It isn't like I can never go back home. It's just one year of my life, I suppose," which now that he met Noah, he wondered if that year would end as quickly as he thought. Could he return to Connecticut for college? He knew he wanted to be around his friends again, but he also felt weird thinking about that life when he now knows Noah. Timothy had to remind himself that he has known Noah all of two days now. It wasn't as if they had known one another for years on end. "Do you miss back East a lot?"

She shrugged, "My entire life is back there, Timothy. My family, friends, the school that I had attended, the little diner that I had met your father in years ago, my childhood home, and the list go on. My life was in Connecticut."

If that were the case, then why on earth did they move? Timothy knew why because his father got a new job. It just seemed weird to suddenly uproot their life out of nowhere, especially when it was a job that his father could have just traveled to. He understood that it would have meant months away, but it would have only been for a year or so. This was his senior year of high school, and he was in a different district in a different state clear across the country.

He got a text message, and it was from Collin. Timothy looked up at his mom, "Collin wants me to get on our live stream."

Ana smiled and nodded, "Dinner will be ready in an hour or so. I've been baking a brisket all day."

"Perfect leftovers for days!" Timothy joked.

"The best kind of leftovers!" Ana joked back. She blew her son a kiss and walked out.

Timothy ran over to his computer and sat down. He logged into the group chat, and Collin logged on. "Hey, man! Is Phillip joining us?" There was something off about Collin's face. He looked kind of sad, but also not really.

"I need to tell you something," Collin admitted.

There was some sort of guilt in his voice. "What's wrong?" Timothy asked.

His friend just sat there for a whole minute and finally took a deep breath. "Tara and I kissed," admitted Collin.

They did what? Timothy thought to himself. How could they do that? Tara was his girlfriend. Timothy thought about that for another second. Tara WAS his girlfriend. Timothy had literally just done more than kiss someone else in the course of eighteen hours. They technically were over but still, "Do you like her?" Timothy finally got it out.

Collin bit his lip for a second, "Yeah, man, I kind of do. I mean, I do a lot. Please don't be mad."

"I'm not. I mean, it's weird because I never really thought you liked Tara." He had to admit, though, that he always wondered if Tara liked Collin. Timothy wasn't angry, just sort of thrown off, "Look, you are one of my best friends. Tara and I might not be together anymore, but she is also one of my best friends. I want you both to be happy."

His friend smiled, "You are taking this a lot better than Phillip and Tara thought you would."

Timothy laughed, "I mean, there might be someone that I like around here, to be honest." He can't believe he just said that out loud.

"No shit. What is her name?" Collin asked.

Could he tell Collin the truth? This was his best friend since before pre-school, "If it turns into something, I'll tell you their name."

Collin smiled even larger than before, "I'm happy that you are at least meeting people. You seemed so miserable yesterday and the past week or so."

Yeah, he really had been. Noah made him feel happy. As he was thinking this, he got a text. It was from Noah. He was outside and looked up at Collin, "Talk this weekend? I've got to go and do a few things."

"Yeah, totally!" Collin said. He waved goodbye and hung up the call.

* * *

Timothy ran out his front door, eager to see the boy he had only seen a little bit ago. He got back into the car that he had spent half the day in. "What's up?" the curly-haired boy asked.

"I managed to get your homework, I mean the stuff that you would have been doing in class today," Noah said with a smile as he handed him a few pieces of paper.

"How did you get this? I mean, we don't have all the same classes together," Timothy pointed out.

Noah laughed, "Oh, well, considering I work in the counseling office, I figured out how to hack into lesson plans a while ago. The school has a really weak system."

Timothy smiled, "Thanks! This will help keep my mom off my back just in case she asks."

"Oh yeah, no problem," he looked at Timothy with reluctance. "I'm sure that you have stuff you need to do, so I'll let you go. I mean, look over this stuff. Maybe catch up on some reading," Timothy really needed to find a club or job. Regardless of whatever he currently had with Noah, he knew very well that he was going to need to find new hobbies independent of him as well. He looked at his house and could see his mother cooking from a distance. "You want to stay for dinner?" Timothy asked, sort of reluctantly and sort of excited at the prospect.

Noah looked nervous, "Sure. Yeah that should he fine."

CHAPTER NINE

NOAH

The inside of Timothy's house was recently renovated. This was a popular trend in this particular part of the city. Older homes were given modern refinements to suit people new to town. It was definitely much larger than Noah's house but only had one bedroom more than his. The major differences were that Timothy had a formal dining room and a spacious living room. The kitchen was slightly large and much more up to date than his own. He had only ever lived in one house, and aside from the fridge dying on them a few years ago, they had never bought new appliances. It was weird to be in a home where he clearly was the cheapest thing inside. Yet, Timothy didn't seem to notice or care. However, his parents might.

"I just got word from your father. He is working late at the office," Ana, Timothy's mother, told her son. She seemed really nice. It was obvious that on top of being a career woman, she was a homemaker and most of the fine details around the house were her doing; she said as much. Right before they walked into the house, Timothy whispered that his mother was a perfectionist and to just go along with whatever she said. It was the only way.

Something smelled really good. Much better than anything that his family ever cooked, which mostly consisted of family-sized frozen meals from his mom's work. None of the Peters family were really big on cooking, even his extended family. Holiday meals were always trivial and an adventure because of this. "It smells amazing, whatever you are making," Noah explained to Mrs. Powell.

Ana smiled, "You're so thin. I'm going to put some meat on your bones after tonight." She smiled as she left the living room to go do something upstairs.

"She tells all my friends that," Timothy explained to him very quickly after she left.

Noah laughed, "She seems really nice. I'd love for you to meet my mom soon. You've obviously met my brother and sister already."

"Oh yeah, they seem nice. I'm sure that your mom is too," Timothy said with a smile as he put his hand close to Noah's.

"Your house is so nice," Noah said. He had probably said it a good ten times. The word he was really looking for was that it looked clean. His own home was clean, but it still looked lived in even after their weekly scrubbings and dustings. This house looked like a showroom.

Timothy shrugged, "It's not as nice as our old house," he said.

This made Noah a little nervous. If this was not up to par with where they used to live, then lord knows how Timothy had felt being at his own house today. "Hopefully, you get to visit Connecticut soon."

"Not until November, which feels like a lifetime from now," Timothy sighed.

Noah frowned. He couldn't imagine leaving the only life he had ever known. Yet, that was exactly his plan once he graduated. He wondered if things would change if he and Timothy were growing as close as it seemed they were. He was still unsure of how close they were at this point.

"You could maybe come up there with us if you wanted," the curly-haired boy said this almost reluctantly.

It was weird to be invited to a different state by someone that he really didn't know all that well. Yet, he knew him much better than most of the people that he had grown up around. "This is just so weird," Noah whispered.

Timothy looked confused, "What do you mean?"

He wondered, "It's just you and I really don't know one another, and yet we do if that makes any sense."

The tall and skinny boy took Noah's hand. He was a bit confused, but the two went into the foyer because, of course, this house had one of those. They went up the stairs, which had dark wood floors against light blue walls. This house belonged in a magazine or something. It didn't belong in Kansas. They went down a hallway that had perfectly hung artwork. Artwork! Not just family photos, but he did spot a photo that was most definitely a young Timothy, and he looked adorable. They finally reached a room at the end of the hall, "Son of a bitch…, this room is twice the size of mine."

"I just realized that we didn't go into your room earlier today," Timothy said with a little smirk on his face. Noah found this sexy.

"Well, yeah, it was kind of messy, unlike yours." Noah noticed that it looked like the bed had recently been moved from one side to another. Even so, this room was weirdly clean. "Why did you take me up here?" Noah asked. While the idea of sex sounded fun right now, he wasn't entirely sure that he wanted to do it while Timothy's mom was home.

The Jewish boy sat on his bed and gestured for him to do the same, "I just wanted to be able to talk a little bit more freely."

While he hadn't planned on having sex, he was a little let down that they really weren't going to fuck. Noah had to admit that he was getting a little horny over the prospect. Oh well, he thought, "Perfect." He sat down next to him on the bed. It was weird to be on a guy's bed, and that guy had feelings of some sort for him.

"Yeah, I'd like for you to come with us if you can for Thanksgiving break, which reminds me, why is that a thing here? Who gets an entire week off for Thanksgiving?" Timothy asked him.

Noah had no idea, and honestly, if he really were to look into why it probably would just be a bigger clusterfuck of false patriotism than this town and state already had. "Who knows…"

So much had changed in such a short period of time. Noah felt like things were going to remain looking up for the rest of the year, he hoped at least.

PART TWO

CHAPTER TEN

TIMOTHY

"Don't forget that we are totally going to go into the city for the parade this year!" Phillip said from the group chat.

Timothy rolled his eyes. "We have been *threatening* to do that for years,» he joked. «I have to get going!» he said as he looked down at a text message. It was from Noah. He was in the driveway. They were going to go to the local store to pick him up some new luggage. Timothy had no idea why on earth he needed it, but the curly-haired boy wasn›t going to argue. They were two days away from descending on Connecticut.

He was about to run downstairs when there was a knock on his door. It was his father. Leo Powell was around the same height as his son. A decent build for a man in his middle age. A slight tan, something that he did not have back in Connecticut, that the family was sure to notice the moment that they got back. "Just wanted to make sure that you were all packed up for Sunday?" his dad asked.

"Yup. I'm just going out for a little bit with Noah," he explained, or, well, reminded his father.

Leo nodded, "That's fine. I have to say I like Noah a little better than those kids you used to hang around back home." He crossed his arms.

Those kids? Collin and Phillip? The two friends that he had since before pre-school? Timothy loved his father, but it always felt like he could never please him. "Well, I'm glad you like him," Timothy said.

His father reached into his pocket and grabbed his wallet. He took out a twenty. "Here. Just so you have some spending money. When we come back from Thanksgiving, it might be time for you to start looking for a job," his father suggested.

"I swear I've applied to every store at the mall," Timothy said. Noah's mom said she could probably get him a job working with her. He just felt like it would have been awkward working for his boyfriend's mom, especially since Cheryl knew they were dating. This was one of the main reasons that Noah's family had seldom interacted with his own, which the Peters family clearly didn't like. "Thanks," Timothy reluctantly told his father, who was clearly looking for thanks.

* * *

It honestly shocked him how cold it was starting to get in Kansas. He had always assumed that Kansas was the south and that it seldom snowed. Yet, it had already snowed twice in a two-week period. Timothy had to break out his winter coat a little before Halloween. He and Noah had gone to some weird barn party with a few friends that they had *both* made. It had been cold, and there was more drug use than either boy had ever thought they would see in a lifetime.

Timothy got into Noah's car. "Hey!" he said. Timothy put his hand on Noah's knee. That was their way of hugging or kissing while still in front of his house.

"Ok... So, you aren't going to say anything?" Noah asked, a little annoyed in tone.

"I have no idea what you are talking about," the Jewish boy said.

Noah pointed to his head, "I got a haircut!"

He couldn't help but laugh, "You get a haircut every other week... It's ok to let it grow a little bit."

"I just want to make a good impression on your friends," Noah explained.

Timothy had promised Noah that when he introduced his friends to him, it would be as his boyfriend. The only thing is that considering

Timothy was still in the closet, he wished he could have come out to them alone first then introduce Noah. It just wasn't something that he felt like he could do over video chat. The other issue was that Timothy was still sort of kind of questioning what he was and wasn't. There were days when he felt like men were all he was attracted to, and then he would see a girl and start getting feelings. It was obvious that he was into guys. There was no question of it, but he was still trying to figure out if he was into girls. He also had to admit a sense of jealousy whenever he would text with Tara or Collin when Collin had Tara with him in their video chats. He had no sexual attraction to Collin. At least he never thought he did. So, the jealousy had to have lied because Collin was now with the girl he had been with for so long. It had never gone to the next level, though with her.

He turned to Noah, "Look, all you have to do is be yourself, and you should be fine. I know you think that I came from money and lived this extravagant life before you. I didn't. Even if I did, I like you for you." They had avoided saying love towards one another. Noah had nonchalantly sprinkled the word into a conversation, but Timothy would just smile. Neither had said it truly out loud as of yet.

"Sasha gave me a bit of an advance so I could have a little bit of spending money. I told her I didn't need it, but she insisted, which I think is code for, here is some money I don't expect it back," Timothy explained. Noah shrugged as he continued to drive. They were just going to go to his moms' work. He had her employee discount.

Timothy needed to pick up a few things as well. He was running out of reading material. Since being in Kansas, he had read through a good two or three novels a week. At first, it was just silly chick-lit books that people would rave about. Then he started to get into crime thrillers for no real reason whatsoever. "Remind me to check out the book section," Timothy said.

"I don't know why you go there when we can just go to Sasha's or the library. With the amount you spend on books, we really should just go to the library," Noah lectured him.

The tall boy couldn't help but laugh, "I just finished up to the part that was already released, in that one series. The newest book came out last week. Your mom said they have it in stock. Sasha won't get it until someone tries selling it for a couple of dollars, after a year of it sitting on someone else's bookshelf collecting dust," Timothy pointed out. The other type of book he had been getting into was romance novels. Not gay romance novels - he had read one or two, but they were just kind of weird. It was the straight romance genre that he was into. They weren't particularly sexy, but he loved the 'will they/won't they' aspect of the books, and you knew damn well they would end up together. Only one of the books ended in the characters not getting together. Sasha had picked that one out for him. Noah made fun of him. The guys that he hung around the school with did as well. He didn't care. A book was more than its cover, which was the most cliché phrase ever.

Noah finally pulled into the parking lot of the store. It was about as packed as usual. It was sadly one of the nicer stores in town. "Ok, I just need new luggage."

"You could literally just empty out your backpack," Timothy rolled his eyes.

"Oh, come on... I just want to fit in," Noah explained.

It still baffled Timothy that Noah was insistent upon him being rich. He wasn't. He clearly had more money than Noah, but again it did not bother him, and it wasn't his money. His dad gave him twenty dollars. He had about a hundred and sixty to his name from saving that twenty each week. It was sad being close to eighteen years old and not having more than a hundred something in the bank. "You'll fit in being your naturally beautiful self, both on the outside and the inside, which is your daily reminder, that the inner beauty of yours is all that matters," Timothy said.

"Just your daily reminder as well, that I didn't fall for your looks, I fell for the fact that you play basketball because I find basketball players sexy," Noah said, all joking.

The two boys got out of the car. Noah started running towards the door. Timothy just laughed. He was freezing himself, but he had no desire to run right now. "You better wait for me to catch up before you run in," he rolled his eyes.

Noah turned around. "Well, come on!" he screamed.

Timothy caught up and patted his boyfriend on the shoulder, "If you weren't so adorable, I'd punch you instead of pat you." Noah was definitely super energetic once you got to know him. It was obvious that the people around him were not aware of this side of the boy, aside from maybe his boss Sasha and his two siblings.

CHAPTER ELEVEN

NOAH

The same repetitive soundtrack that had been playing for the last three years blared at his mom's store. It was so brightly lit and always smelled like makeup and cheap perfume, which Noah secretly loved. It was a change from whatever the rest of the town smelled like, which was ironic considering the entire town shopped here for one thing or another.

"I think that the luggage is going to be over here," Timothy gestured.

"Um, I believe that my mother is the manager of this store," Noah reminded him.

Timothy put his hands in the store, "Ok, Mister Son of the Manager, where is the luggage section?"

The blonde boy looked around, "Probably in the same direction you just pointed to." Timothy rolled his eyes at Noah, which Noah always found sexy. He loved it when Timothy got annoyed with him.

After their first sexual experiences together, the two boys had agreed to playthings very slow. Noah hated it. The only time he really got to see anything was during gym class, which wasn't very much. He admittedly tried to chase him a few minutes longer during class in order to get Timothy to shower. It worked sometimes but not very often.

The only part that really was a downfall was the fact that he and Timothy were only best friends in public places. It was only in private that they were dating. This wasn't the worst thing ever. It wasn't as if Noah didn't have common sense. They weren't going to be making out at school, or they would be expelled. A normal couple would just be told to break it up. They would be accused of having a hard-core gang bang in the common area if they even pecked each other on the lips. It was just that he wished they could at least be open.

Timothy had made friends with some semi-decent people at school that never would have given Noah the time of day before. It was weird that these people who had either ignored or made fun of him his whole life were now ok with him. It was just ridiculous that it took the perception from a *straight* athlete, who thought it was alright, so it must have been ok. It was totally pathetic in his mind. It wasn't Timothy's fault at all, though. Noah, however, had yet to really address his feelings on the subject yet.

It only took a few minutes for them to find the luggage. Timothy was, of course, right. "I don't want to hear it. You are always right, and that is the last time I will admit to it," Noah proclaimed.

His boyfriend smiled at him. "I know I'm always right. So, stop arguing all the time," he winked playfully.

"Do you like this red one or the black one better?" Noah asked.

There was a purple one that Timothy found, "I like this one best, obviously."

Noah picked it up, "Oh, I totally forgot about your purple obsession."

"It's just a very neutral color," Timothy explained.

"You know when I was younger in music class, we would do ribbon day each year. It was just twirling ribbons to different music," Noah told him.

The curly-haired boy nodded, "I think we did something similar."

"Well anyway, I picked the purple ribbon. I didn't really think much of it, but some girl stated it was a girl color," Noah said. Noah would often remember things from elementary school that he did. He would sit with the girls at lunch. He would insist on getting the pink ball during recess. As he grew into his teens, he would purposely avoid anything that was perceived as feminine. It was funny that after coming out, he still felt the need to hide in the corner when it came to those supposedly feminine items.

The boyfriend just laughed, "That is just ignorance at its best. A color doesn't mean anything. Well, actually, purple is associated with being gay but still…"

Noah looked at him, "So, you would wear pink to Thanksgiving dinner?"

The taller boy thought about it for a second, "A pink button-down? Sure. An entirely pink outfit? No. I would look absolutely ridiculous. You go for it, though. I support you!" as he started to laugh.

Things like this would sometimes get to Noah. Timothy seemed very standoffish about anything considered counterculture, which for whatever reason, included the different colors. It wasn't like he was going to ask him to wear heels, but even so, it wasn't that big a deal. Which again, Noah wasn't asking, and he himself had no desire himself, but if either boy randomly decided to, then Noah wouldn't blink an eye. Timothy would, though… "I'll get the purple one for you then," Noah said.

"I'm not going to be the one using it, though," Timothy reminded him.

"Yes, but as you pointed out, it is just a color," Noah explained.

Timothy smiled, "You are adorable."

He hoped he was, "You are too." He really was. His smile was infectious. Noah wished it wasn't, but it totally was. Noah was slowly falling in love with this boy for real. He would find something new to be in love with every single day, and it was the greatest thrill of his life. "So, then Collin and Phillip are your two best friends, right?" Noah asked.

"And Tara. Yeah, we were the four musketeers back home, really," Timothy explained with a smile.

"Right and Tara… So, then Phillip is the cuter one, and Collin is the funnier one, right?" Noah was trying to make sure that he would be able to fit in with this new group. If they were important to Timothy, then it was his new mission to make sure that Timothy's friends and extended family all liked him.

His boyfriend sighed, "I suppose that Phillip is the cuter one. I consider him a brother, so I never really thought about it. Collin is just a bunch of bad dad jokes, but I suppose. You seem to think the things he says are funny. He and Tara have been dating for a while now."

Noah smiled, "Cool. So, am I going to get to see where you went to high school as well?"

"If you really feel the need to see it, sure," Timothy explained.

As the two continued to awkwardly talk about Connecticut. Cheryl walked over, "Oh, the purple one? I would have pegged you for the blue one."

"He's trying to impress me for no reason again, Cheryl." Timothy put his hands on his hips as he said it. Noah was getting a little concerned with how much his mother and boyfriend seemed to get along. Yes, in a perfect world, he always wanted that to be a case but even so. It was just downright weird.

"I'm just trying to fit in on the East Coast. I've never been before." Noah had to admit that he imagined a universe where the East Coast was where he ended up in the Fall. He wanted to follow Timothy and knew that was where he would go. Noah wasn't stupid; Timothy wasn't going out West. Sure, it was a completely different idea than he originally had, but there was New York and Philadelphia. Plus, Noah had to admit that he enjoyed having seasons, which Timothy insisted Kansas had only three, and he was missing out on the fourth.

Cheryl patted her son's back, "Oh, just be yourself."

Timothy nodded, "That's what I keep telling him. He just won't listen."

It was easier said than done, which was something that he wished Timothy would acknowledge sometimes.

Timothy's parents were probably the only people in town who had no idea he was gay. He often wondered if they did know. He really didn't do much to hide it. The real question was if they knew their son was too. Noah had no issue with Timothy still being in the closet. He just didn't understand what was taking so long to come out. His parents didn't really seem to be homophobic. Noah did have to admit that Timothy's religion, which he was active in, was very confusing on all matters of just about everything. He knew they had similar views on homosexuality, yet his parents did not give off the same vibe that maybe a Christian-based household would about anything.

His mother did mention him finding a nice Jewish girl. That was something that Noah couldn't really give her on either front. Yet, Noah was interested in learning more about it. He was almost certain that their week in Connecticut would be filled with many cultural differences in that regard.

"Fine. I will go with the blue bag," Noah said.

"Great. I'll bring it up front and have it ready for you when you are both done window shopping. The girls on cash know to use my discount. Love you." His mother kissed him on the forehead like she always did. She walked away, shaking her head and laughing.

The two boys continued to venture down the aisles. Noah knew that Timothy wanted to look at the books. "I'm working on a new story right now," Noah said.

Timothy looked at him as they walked, "Wonderful. Am I going to be able to read this one?"

Noah sighed, "I just want to make sure it is perfect."

"Well then, can I read the last one that you were working on? I'm sure it is perfect by now," Timothy said as he gave Noah a smart-ass look. Noah smacked him on the shoulder.

"It's not perfect yet either," Noah explained. He just wasn't comfortable having anyone read his stuff yet. Noah wrote for himself, and while he didn't mind criticism or suggestions in theory, he didn't want to share stories that were so personal with the world. His books were not meant for the shipping communities or fangirl slash boy fandoms. They were meant for his own personal taste in mind. It was also weird because he wrote stories for straight people, which people never understood, especially when he spoke with people online. They couldn't possibly understand why a queer guy would ever want to write about straight people. It was simple...., until recently, he had been living vicariously through the cautious lens of straight couples. In contrast, gay guys were a different world entirely, one he only really knew about on the surface. "You just have to give me time," Noah said.

The taller boy stopped in the middle of the aisle. "Noah, I don't care if it is the worst story ever. I'm obviously not going to be a jerk about it if it is. I just want you to be the best you can be. If this is what you want to do for a living, then eventually someone will have to read your stories."

He knew. Lord, did he ever know. "Ok. I'll let you read one of my stories during the break. I don't want you to tell me anything positive or negative about it until we get back, though," Noah said.

The boyfriend smiled, "Perfect. You are going to be nagging me the entire week. Sounds like a plan." Noah once again smacked him, "Don't act like it won't happen."

* * *

Later on, that evening, after he dropped off Timothy, he sat in his bedroom and sighed. He had legit already picked out all his outfits three times over. One of the reasons he didn't want to use his backpack was that he knew damn well; he needed options. Everyone could say what they wanted, but he was going to be an outsider in a group of people with pre-established relationships. Noah wanted to get to know these people, but he was just a quiet person until you got to know him.

There was a knock on his bedroom door. "Come in," Noah said.

Brick walked in, looking like he had been beaten with a bag of....well, bricks. "Hey," Brick said.

"Why do you look so terrible?" Noah didn't even try to sugarcoat it. His brother looked rough.

His brother sat down on his bed next to him, "I don't think it is going to last between Amber and I."

Noah's heart started to fall all over the place. "Wait... what? Why?" If this was a year ago, Noah would be breaking out the balloons, but Amber was going to deliver the child within the next month or so. Things were a little different. "What about the baby?"

"Obviously, I'm going to take care of the baby. I just don't see a future with her. I know you don't like her, and I know mom doesn't either. It's just I'd rather your opinion than hers," Brick explained.

This was really the first time ever that his brother had ever come to him for advice. "Well, no… I don't like her. I also don't like her family. My future niece or nephew is going to grow up with a warped set of values in that household." Noah knew damn well that if Amber's parents had their way, he probably would never be able to see his future niece or nephew. It was just a reality that the Peters family had all been avoiding given the situation's overall shock value.

Brick nodded, "I think she has been seeing someone else away at school. I should be in school. There I said it. I'm busting my ass for a child that again I want to be there for, but I can't even trust Amber anymore."

"Honestly, when did you? Let's be honest, you thought she was a hot piece of ass, and you went for her," Noah just bluntly stated.

"Where on earth did that come from?" Brick started laughing.

Noah honestly had no idea, "Look, don't stay with her because of the child. Just please don't be a deadbeat."

His brother sighed, "If I have to take her to court, I will. I'm not saying that we are breaking up. I'd like to give it one more chance."

This meant that there was at least another six months of pleasantries with Amber if things didn't work out. Brick was stubborn. It only took this long for him to realize the girl was not a good person.

"I need your advice now," Noah said.

"Does this have anything to do with the fact that every piece of clothing you own is currently on the floor?" His brother looked around, a bit confused.

It wasn't all out. He didn't really consider underwear or socks. Though now that he was thinking about it, he probably should. The wrong pair of socks could really piss someone off. "I just really want to fit into Timothy's life," said Noah.

"Noah, you are going to Connecticut - that's his old life," Brick pointed out.

He didn't get it. "Well, it is going to be his life again after graduation," said Noah.

"You still have some time before that becomes a reality. You need to just be yourself with him," Brick explained to his younger brother.

"I'll try…" Noah threw his head into a pillow, stressed out.

CHAPTER TWELVE

TIMOTHY

The plane ride started positively. That was until Noah handed him a giant wad of papers and told him he could start reading. It was honestly the most adorable thing he could have done. Timothy's parents had chosen seats in a different section entirely, so they had a tiny bit of privacy. He still didn't get very close with Noah out of fear someone could be watching. When Timothy started to read the story, he had to admit it wasn't terrible. It definitely needed some help, though. There was a lot to go with it before he could give a final judgment. Noah continued to ask him questions the entire flight, to the point where Timothy finally pretended to take a nap, which turned into a real one.

On their ride to Timothy's grandmother's house, Noah had been silent. Everyone had been silent, but Noah's silence concerned him. It was obvious that he was scared out of his mind over this new experience. It was the most cliché thing that he could possibly think, but they weren't in Kansas anymore. While Timothy knew damn well that Noah had never really been comfortable there, it was a comfort zone compared to this new world.

He had to imagine that Noah was rethinking a lot of things in his head. Some of which probably involved himself. He didn't think that there was anything negative going on. He just didn't know what to think.

As they arrived at his grandma's, it was a large jolt of memories. His own childhood home was only a few blocks away. Noah had stated he wanted to see that as well. Since they still owned the property, there was a fifty/fifty chance they would actually be able to go inside it. The person who was renting it chose to buy themselves out of their lease. He just wasn't sure if his dad would let him get the keys. It was clear that his father was uncomfortable for a different set of reasons.

After a million hugs and a good hour of discussing all their new realities, Timothy took Noah to one of the guest rooms. This one happened to be in the attic, which meant that they would have complete privacy.

"She seems nice. Your grandmother, I mean," Noah said. He was clearly still in his head.

"Yes, which means you clearly have nothing to worry about, so stop thinking whatever it is you are thinking!" Timothy screamed at him in a whisper voice.

Noah sunk down on the bed. He then looked around… "Um, there is only one bed up here… did you bring a sleeping bag?"

It finally sunk in. This was the first time the two boys would be spending the night together. What was even weirder was the fact that they would potentially be sharing a queen-sized bed. Timothy couldn't imagine that anyone would question it. After all, no one knew that the two boys were dating. "I could sleep on the ground if it made you feel more comfortable," Timothy said. He looked at Noah, whose smile sunk at that suggestion. "Or we could share a bed…"

"I have to admit that I prefer that concept to the first suggestion," Noah explained.

Timothy rolled his eyes. He felt a vibration in his pocket and took out his phone. "Phillip's on his way to pick us up. We are going to meet Collin and Tara up at my old school," Timothy explained.

"I get to meet your friends!" Noah said with excitement and reluctance in the same breath.

"Yeah, you do," Timothy smiled. He looked at his watch, "We just have to be quiet as we walk downstairs. Grandmother is watching her stories right now. She is obsessed over that one with the redhead that's always marrying her cousin."

Noah looked confused, "Redhead, who always marries her cousin?"

Timothy laughed, "Yeah, I don't know, soaps are not my thing. She has been watching since the late '60s. Don't get her started, or she will start going on and on about Clifton and Dallas. Again, no idea what she is talking about."

* * *

Phillip's car made its way to the driveway. Timothy had to admit that he liked the fact that it was Phillip picking them up because Phillip's car was a piece of shit. Timothy knew this because it used to be his car. "Hey, man!" Timothy said with a smile. He grabbed Noah by the arm because he was clearly nervous.

"I want the new guy in the front seat," Phillip stated.

"Wait... what?" Noah asked.

Phillip laughed, "It's the best way to get to know you!"

This was what he loved about Phillip. He was no-nonsense and knew how to make everyone feel wanted. "Go for it, Noah!" Timothy told his boyfriend. He could tell Noah was uncomfortable, but it was a great way to get him out of his shell.

He begged Phillip to take the long way as it had felt like forever since he had been home. They passed by his old house. Apparently, Phillip had been put in charge of keeping the grass cut. He had been complaining the other week that he was about to lose a source of income thanks to the seasons changing.

"So, Noah, are you from Kansas originally?" Phillip asked.

The questions kept on coming for Noah, which Timothy couldn't help but laugh about.

When they finally stopped, it felt so surreal. He almost felt like he was missing his backpack or forgot his basketball shoes for practice. It then hit him; this would be the first year he wouldn't play on the team. Timothy took a deep breath. His life had changed forever, all because his father is a stubborn man. However, it did bring Noah to his life, though. That was all that mattered at the moment. Then she walked towards the car.

"Tara!" Timothy said as he ran out of the car and into her arms.

The blonde-haired beauty smiled, "I've missed you so much, Timmy!" she laughed.

CHAPTER THIRTEEN

NOAH

What in the hell was going on? Noah thought as he watched his boyfriend hug this girl. It shouldn't be bothering him, and yet it was. Noah heard for months about how amazing Phillip and Collin were. Tara was just an add on most of the time. Yet, he gave Phillip a high-five when reuniting, and this Tara girl was practically dry humping him in public. It was worse than Lily and Ned at that one dance two years ago.

Noah stormed over to his boyfriend but then realized that to these people, they were not dating because Timothy was not out. He just stood there with a blank expression.

His boyfriend turned around. "Oh… Tara. This is Noah. We have gotten really close while I've been away."

While he has been away? It was almost as if he was saying that in a way that meant he would be returning tomorrow for good. Noah went from being excited and scared to be introduced to Timothy's old life, to feeling very pissed off very quickly. What on earth was going on? Why was this random girl pissing him off so much? Why was she still holding on to him?

"It's nice to meet you!" Tara said with a smile.

Another boy with short curly hair walked over. He was slightly taller than Timothy, which threw Noah off, "It's good to see you, bro."

"Collin!" Timothy said out loud.

Phillip soon joined the other two boys and Tara. Noah was now the odd one out, and it only took all of three minutes for this to escalate. "So, why don't you show me around?" Noah suggested to Timothy.

"Actually, I can do it!" Phillip said, grabbing his hand.

"Yeah, that sounds perfect! It will give me some time with Timmy!" Tara said with this obnoxious, almost dense tone about her.

* * *

Phillip walked Noah all around the campus. It was definitely smaller than Wichita West. Yet, it had a certain charm about it. Noah was still pissed off, though, at whatever he had just viewed in terms of Tara and Timothy. That boy had a lot of explaining to do when they were in private. Phillip had quickly filled him in on everything.

"So, then how long have Collin and Tara been seeing each other then?"

"Well, they saw each other for a month or so. They aren't really together anymore. Tara hasn't really gotten over Tim," Phillip explained as they walked down the hall.

Why on earth were these people allowed to call his boyfriend by nicknames? Yet, he had to refer to him strictly as Timothy. Which is what he claimed to prefer. "Yet, Collin seems ok with this?" Noah pointed out. He seemed to be just as excited as Phillip had been.

Phillip laughed, "I mean, it isn't like there aren't other girls for Collin. Do you have a girlfriend back home?" he asked.

"I'm not into girls," Noah said. His eyes widened. "Fuck..." Noah said out loud as well. That's how he would have answered it had some stranger asked him, and technically speaking, Phillip was a stranger.

The light-skinned Japanese boy brushed his hair back. "Oh, wow, really?" he asked.

Good lord. He was already pissed off, and now he was about to get gay-bashed, "Yup. Is that going to be a problem?"

"No... Not at all," Phillip said. He crossed his arms.

Noah couldn't read his facial expression, "You sure about that?"

"Yeah." He looked to see if anyone was around. "I don't like girls either."

Noah blinked, "Wait. What?" This was supposed to be Timothy's best friend in the world, and yet neither boy had ever happened to mention to the other that they were both gay? Though looking at Timothy, he was questioning if he was actually gay right this moment. Clearly, Timothy had been into Noah, but he really never made it a point to really state his love or attraction to other men in the sense of someone being attractive on TV or anything. Yet, he seemed to have some weird obsession with certain female celebrities in a non-fan like way but more of a horny teenage boy way. Noah always shrugged it off since it usually was when they were at school around other guys that were straight. Yet, now here he was with someone that was supposed to be Timothy's lifelong best friend, and he admitted to a total stranger that he didn't like women but men as well. "Does Timothy know this about you?" Noah asked.

Phillip stopped in his tracks. "Uh no… I've only recently come out to my own family. They are ok with it, at least on the surface, it seems." This was normally code for you do you, but don't bring that home.

"I don't think that Timothy would have an issue with it," Noah said, a little annoyed in tone. He wasn't sure why he was annoyed with this boy that was coming out to him. None of this was his fault. Noah sighed, "I'm happy that you felt comfortable enough to come out to me."

"I mean, I don't really know you, but you seem cool," Phillip explained. He got a little closer to Noah.

Although he wasn't really sure where he stood with Timothy at the moment, he was still with him as far as he knew, "I have a boyfriend…" Noah blurted out.

Phillip looked up, "Oh. That's cool. I'm sure he is a lucky guy."

"Oh, he has no idea just how lucky he is," Noah said, frustrated. Noah needed a minute alone with Timothy to sort this out.

As they continued to walk down the hall awkwardly, they finally spotted Timothy, who was now only with Collin. Tara was nowhere around. Good. Noah walked right over to Timothy without a smile on his face, "Can we chat for a minute?"

"I'll be back in a sec!" Timothy said to his two best friends.

The two boys walked around the corner, where no one seemed to be around. "What on earth is going on around here?" he asked.

"What do you mean?" Timothy asked, confused.

"Uh... your ex-girlfriend who is clearly still in love with you," Noah said as he crossed his arms.

Timothy turned pale white. Which was unflattering considering he already was rather white, "So, Phillip told you?"

"Among other things..." Which wasn't his place to say anything. Though he hoped for Phillip's sake that he tells Timothy before he leaves because it was clearly something the two boys needed to hash out. "Why didn't you tell me about her?"

Timothy sighed, "I don't know..."

"Are you gay?" Noah asked.

Timothy turned around for a second, "I mean... I like you a lot. I want you in ways that I've never wanted someone else, including Tara."

Noah's stomach sank. That was all he needed to hear. "Ok... I'm glad to hear." He didn't care if Timothy was gay or bi or whatever. So, long as he liked and potentially loved him, that was all he cared about.

"Just because we are here doesn't mean that I'm automatically in love with Tara. Are there still feelings? Yes, but it never felt like it feels with you." Timothy sunk to the floor, sliding against lockers. Noah joined him.

This week was just going to be full of surprises. Noah supposed it was better that they had this conversation now and not later, though. He had to admit that actually speaking with him made him a little less pissed off. Just a little bit, though, but it was hard to stay mad at Timothy. He had only just started exploring his sexuality, which wasn't something that he had thought much of.

Noah got into his head, which was never a good thing. He had to wonder if he was just a stop on the way to Timothy exploring his sexuality. The blond boy turned to his boyfriend, "I'm in this for the long run. Can you promise me that you have that mindset as well?"

Timothy looked at him for a minute with a frown and then smiled, "Noah, I don't want anyone else but you. I have no idea where next fall will take us, but I know that this fall was one of the best times of my life ever."

CHAPTER FOURTEEN

TIMOTHY

Everything he just said was true. Yet, he couldn't help but feel old feelings burst all over the place as he thought about Tara. It was so easy to fall back into old ways with that girl. It was easy to go back to the old ways, just being around his old friends and old surroundings. Timothy missed this place. The real question was, did he miss this place more than he liked Noah?

At the end of the day, Noah was a great guy. Probably one of the best people he had ever met. Yet, Noah wanted to live on the West Coast. He'd rather stay in Connecticut. There was definitely an argument for New York but Long Island, not Manhattan or Brooklyn. He just wasn't into the concept of some loud and excessive world, which Noah seemed to thrive on, whereas Timothy liked quiet, but not Kansas quiet.

"So, what are we doing with your friends tonight?" Noah asked.

"Just hanging out. I want them to be your friends too," Timothy explained. He really did. If this was going to work out, then they all had to like one another. He also had no choice, "I'm going to have to come out to them."

Noah looked at him and smiled, "I will be there for you as much or as little as you want me to be there when you do."

* * *

Timothy knew that he needed to do this alone but also tell Collin and Phillip before Tara. Noah went to do some writing in the library but said he was a text away, and he would run as fast as he could.

The curly-haired boy looked at his two best friends, "I have something I need to tell you both."

"You're moving back?" Collin asked with a smile.

"Well, now whatever he was going to say is just not going to be as big," Phillip said, bopping Collin on the forehead.

Timothy loved these guys, "I'm just going to come out and say it… I'm into guys." That was the most honest he could be. "I don't know if I'm gay, but I definitely am not straight."

It took a moment of silence, but Phillip hugged him. Collin followed. "I don't care if you are into trees," Collin said.

"Well, unfortunately for you, I'm not," Timothy said, giving him a weird look.

"Well, damn because I am!" Collin joked.

Phillip looked at him for a second, "You're dating Noah, aren't you?"

This comment threw Timothy for a loop, but he smiled, "Yeah, I am."

"He seems like a good guy. If he ever hurts you though, he will have me on his case," Phillip said, crossing his arms.

There was something about how Phillip was taking this that felt weird, but Timothy just shrugged it off. "He's a great guy. He's the reason that I've been able to accept myself," Timothy said.

"You could have told us," Collin said. There was this hurt sound in his voice.

Timothy had known these guys since elementary school. Part of him knew he always could, but a small part of him feared what would happen if they didn't accept him. "You two are like brothers to me. It's just hard to tell people a flaw about yourself," Timothy said.

"A flaw? That's not a flaw! A flaw is how weak you are on the court!" Phillip joked.

The tall one rolled his eyes. "Oh, because you are so good at the game." This was all great. He was happy that his friends were ok with this. He just wished that he had told them a lot sooner. Timothy had to wonder if things would be different if he had told them a year or so ago. Only because one; they were younger, and two; it wasn't as if he was going back to be leaving them at that point. They would have had to live with the revelation on a daily basis.

There were still a few loose ends. Tara and his family, both equally important people, needed to know. Why did he have to date his childhood friend? If Tara had been some random girl, she would have eventually found out through social media maybe a decade later, and it would have been over with. It just couldn't be simple. "Any chance you and Tara will get back together?" he asked Collin.

Collin frowned, "I doubt it. She is still pretty big on you, which is cool. I mean, she is a great girl, but it clearly wasn't meant to be in that way."

Not the answer he was looking for. Timothy sighed, "Oh boy…" As he continued to gather his thoughts, he noticed that someone was hiding behind the corner. "Noah, you can come out now."

The blond boy walked out from behind some lockers, "I already was out. It was you who just did with your friends."

Phillip laughed at this, "He has a point, dude."

"How much did you hear of that conversation?" Timothy crossed his arms.

"Enough," Noah said with a smile.

Collin walked over to Noah, "I don't see it… What do you see in my boy Timothy, Noah?"

Noah laughed, "I don't know… I guess a lot." He smiled at Timothy. It was so dreamy. That was the only way that Timothy could describe it to himself.

"So, then, I assume that the two of you are going to come to the party tomorrow night before Thanksgiving Day?" Phillip asked.

The two boyfriends looked at one another. "What party?" Timothy asked.

"I'm throwing one," Collin explained.

This was the first time that he had heard about it. "Yeah, I guess it will be fun to see everyone else," Timothy explained.

CHAPTER FIFTEEN

NOAH

It was difficult to find a decent outfit to wear for the party. Timothy was insistent that he could literally just wear what he had on, but Noah wanted to make a decent impression around these strangers. Noah never felt like a cowboy in Kansas, but it was a completely different story amongst these Connecticut people. Timothy had no comment and just sat on their shared bed, waiting for him to make up his mind. "It should only be a few more minutes," Noah explained.

"Well, you have about five. Phillip is back on his way. Collin and Tara are with him," Timothy explained.

"Do you plan on telling her tonight?" Noah asked. He sat down on the bed.

His boyfriend sat up a little bit, "I think it is for the best. I hope you realize that just because she is my ex doesn't make her a bad person. This is definitely a weird situation for you, I know."

Noah shrugged, "I guess that I just never really took bisexuality at face value. I believe it exists a hundred percent. I don't care that you are." He really didn't. All he cared about was the fact that they were together. Noah knew all the tasteless jokes and warnings. Bisexuals can't make up their minds and can't be trusted. Noah knew that Timothy only had eyes for him. If he found women attractive too, that was great. He was secure enough to know he didn't have to worry. At least in theory.

The two boys looked at one another in the eyes. Timothy pulled Noah down on the bed. They started to get closer and closer until they were holding one another. Noah rolled on top of Timothy and started to kiss him on the lips. He would slowly separate each kiss, wanting them to last forever. Noah opened his eyes. "I love you," he blurted out. He rolled off of his boyfriend. "I mean…"

Timothy put his finger on Noah's lips, "I love you too."

"Really? You aren't just saying that in the moment?" Noah asked. He definitely meant it when he said it but didn't want Timothy to think he owed him a response himself.

The boyfriend sat up in bed again, "You and I are perfect together. I love you." He looked into his eyes, and Noah could tell that Timothy was honest.

Things were becoming more and more real as their relationship had gone on. Hearing Timothy say that he loved Noah, though, made things just even more official. Noah honestly was ready to change his plans for the fall if need be. This wasn't a bad place to live. He could manage it. "So, let's get going to that party," said Noah.

"Don't you want to change forty more times?" Timothy joked.

Noah stood up, "Oh, please, I look fine. It's you that needs some genuine pointers on how to dress," he teased his boyfriend.

* * *

It was a typical high school party, but different. They were at someone's house as the parents were away for the week, which Noah had to admit sounded dreadful considering that it was the week of Thanksgiving. A party back home would have been at a barn or in the woods somewhere. At least the few that he had been to that were in the same vein as this. A bunch of girls in revealing clothes were standing in one corner. A bunch of girls in less revealing clothes in a separate corner gossiping about one another: and the boys were all scattered talking with either girls or each other but more than likely not in a romantic sense. There was liquor, but no one knew where it came from. People were getting high outside, and of course, there were rumblings of people doing harder drugs somewhere, but no one knew who was doing them or who was supplying, which meant that everyone knew.

Timothy stayed close with Noah, mostly because Noah refused to leave his side. There were definitely other strangers to this group around, but Noah doubted that any of them were so far removed. A rival high school was different than someone from a different state entirely. The blonde boy had to admit he wasn't really nervous otherwise, though. The only thing that he really was concerned about was Tara. Noah believed that Timothy loved him, but the fact was he could still very well love Tara, and Tara still had no idea he was gay. This Tara girl was nowhere to be found, though. Which both relieved him and made him curious.

Noah thought too soon, and a girl walked through the crowd. She seemed to be more than a little confident, and this girl was, of course, Tara.

"Hey, Timothy!" she said, giggling with a smile on her face. Noah didn't know how he was supposed to feel towards this girl. She was Timothy's childhood best friend, along with Collin and Phillip. That didn't change the fact that the two did date, and the two did have major feelings for one another at one point, which were clearly still shared, at least on one side. Noah was getting annoyed and dizzy, thinking about Timothy and Tara.

Timothy, of course, smiled like he was about to start kissing her in front of everyone. "Hey!" he said. Timothy looked at Noah. "I'm going to talk with Tara for a bit. I promise that I will be back in a little bit," he explained.

Noah nodded. He understood that the two needed to talk. He also understood that he needed to explain certain things to her. Noah just wished that he could be there with his boyfriend when it happened. "Ok, I'll see you in a little bit," Timothy said. Noah noted that Tara didn't really acknowledge his existence during either of their interactions.

"So, you and Timothy are happy?" Noah turned around to find Phillip.

"I'm sorry I didn't tell you earlier," Noah felt guilty. "It just wasn't my place to tell you."

Phillip sighed, "No man, I get it. I'm honestly happy that Timothy has a boyfriend who wouldn't go spreading his secrets around.

This was a relief. He felt bad for Phillip, "Why didn't you come out to Timothy when he came out?"

"It was his moment. Why should I ruin it?" Phillip asked.

He had a point but then realized something, "You need to tell him now. When are you going to be around him again and Collin at the same time? I mean, I hope for all of your sake soon, but still."

Timothy's friend had his head down, "I know... I mean, my family knows already. It's just you never know how people will react."

"I doubt that Timothy will have an issue with it. I also doubt that Collin will if he didn't have an issue with Timothy," Noah put into perspective.

Phillip grabbed Noah's hand, "Come on, let's go find Timmy! We can tell him together and then let it down gently to Collin that he is the only straight guy in the group."

The two boys rushed upstairs. Noah had slightly forgotten that Timothy was with Tara but also slightly remembered and didn't really care. He wanted to be around his boyfriend. Phillip seemed to know where he was going. Clearly, this wasn't the first party thrown at this house. They reached the end of the hall, and Phillip opened the door. He immediately slammed it shut. "No one is in there..."

"What?" Noah asked. He wanted to see for himself because he was genuinely confused. The blond boy opened the door himself. There on the bed two seventeen-year old's were completely naked and having sex. One of these people was definitely Tara. The other... Timothy. His boyfriend turned as he realized the door was opened.

"Noah this... Well... Fuck!" Timothy said.

CHAPTER SIXTEEN

TIMOTHY

How on earth was this happening? Why was this happening? When he and Tara had gone upstairs, things were awkward for a number of reasons. She had been trying to get his pants off before they even sat down. Then he tried explaining to her that he was bisexual, and then she just started to kiss him. It just felt like old times, and things got really heated really quickly. This wasn't how things were supposed to go down. Yet, here they were. He cheated on Noah. He cheated on the most beautiful human being, both inside and out.

"How could you do this to me?" Noah whispered.

Timothy honestly had no idea. It was never his intention to sleep with Tara. He wanted to be with Noah. He had planned on using the condom in his wallet with him that night after the party. Things were going perfectly, and then this happened. "I'm so sorry," said Timothy.

"Um, let's give them a little time to get dressed, Noah," Phillip said.

He had no idea why Phillip was with him. Yet he was a tiny bit thankful that his friend was taking the lead in playing damage control. Timothy needed to explain himself, but he wasn't going to do it naked. Phillip took Noah away and closed the door.

"What the hell is going on?" Tara asked as she sat up in the bed, "Your friend from Kansas is a little clingy."

"He's not my friend…he's my boyfriend," Timothy turned to her. He wasn't sure if he should sit down, or if he should start getting dressed or what.

Tara looked at him for the longest second, "I'm sorry, what did you just say to me?"

"Tara, I'm bisexual. That's why I wanted to talk with you."

His former girlfriend just kept looking at him. It lasted a lot longer than he expected. "You're bisexual? You've been cheating on me with a guy? Do I need to get tested?" Tara asked.

He couldn't believe that she just asked that, "What the fuck Tara? Tested for what? AIDS? I've only messed around with him. I just lost my virginity to you." He couldn't believe what had just come out of her mouth. He knew now it was time to leave. Timothy needed to go speak with Noah. The curly-haired boy found his clothes and started to put them on.

"I didn't mean it like that, Timmy. Why wouldn't you tell me you were bisexual? I'm just confused. I'm hurt," Tara explained.

If she had reacted differently to the news, he might have been less offended, and yet her response was to ask if she needed to be tested. "I'll see you later," he said as he slipped his shoe on. He stormed out the door leaving her by herself.

There was part of him that wanted to stay with her and hash things out. It was apparent that the two of them had unfinished business for a lot of reasons. It was obvious that he still liked her, and Timothy knew that coming back home. He should have been more honest with her and Noah. The issue was, though, he technically wasn't with Tara anymore. They had broken up. It didn't change the fact that he just cheated on Noah with her.

When he went down the hallway, his heart was pounding so hard. This should not have happened. Yet, in a way, it almost felt like it needed to. Was it closure? Timothy had always pictured the person he would lose his virginity to would be Tara. Yet, then he met Noah, and they could hardly keep their hands off one another that second day. Timothy wanted him the moment that he saw him. It took a lot more time for him to ease up to the idea of being with Tara in a sexual way. It confirmed a lot, though. He enjoyed it. At least he enjoyed the feeling. Maybe it was just because sex felt good. Maybe that was what he was feeling? Timothy felt nothing but guilt now.

He made his way down the staircase and found a living room filled with underage drinking. "Where are Noah and Phillip?"

"I don't know," Collin said, a little confused and maybe a little tipsy.

"Dude… I fucked up big time," Timothy said. It took everything for him to not burst into tears.

Collin looked at him and gestured for him to walk outside with him. The two did. Clearly, Phillip's car was gone, "What's wrong?" Timothy asked.

There really wasn't any way of not explaining things, "I just hooked up with Tara… it was by accident."

His best friend looked him in the eye, "I thought you were dating that Noah guy?"

"I was… I am. I think I am. Fuck!" Timothy screamed out, as he sunk to the ground.

Collin followed suit with him, "It will work out. You and Noah seem close. You just… well, I don't know."

Of course, he didn't. Collin had never cheated on someone. Yet, Timothy just did. Timothy fucked up so royally. There was no coming back from this.

CHAPTER SEVENTEEN

NOAH

Could he forgive him? Should he forgive him? What in the actual fuck did he just walk into back there? Noah had already started sobbing twice over. Phillip asked him if he wanted to be dropped off at Timothy's grandmother's house. Noah didn't want to. He had nowhere else to go, though. It wasn't like he could get on a plane, which made him realize that he would be stuck here for the rest of the week. They had a long way to go. Phillip suggested they go back to his house. He apparently lived with a single mother in a modest home. Apparently, modest meant ranch style because this house was definitely not modest.

Phillip handed him a glass of water, "Just in case you get thirsty. You're breathing heavily. It might help," he sat down next to him in bed.

"Why are you helping me out? I'm a stranger. On top of that, I'm Timothy's boyfriend or was, or I don't know," Noah reminded him.

The boy shrugged, "This is going to sound really weird given the circumstances, but I feel like I'm doing it because Timothy does care about you. It's a really poor choice of words, I know, but yeah," he admitted.

It was sad, but Noah knew exactly what he meant. Timothy did care about him. Noah believed him one hundred and ten percent when he said he loved him earlier. Noah still believed it. His theory, though, was also a hundred percent correct. Timothy still loved Tara. It was a question of who he loved more if Noah could even forgive him. "Is he worth forgiving?" Noah asked.

"I mean, he is one of my best friends in the world. I'm obligated to say yes," Phillip shrugged.

"Yes, I realize that. But like if you weren't his best friend, would you be telling me the same thing?" Noah asked.

Phillip shuffled a bit, clearly uncomfortable, "I don't think you need to forgive him a hundred percent right away. I do think you need to take things into perspective. How much do you care about him? Can you go on without him?"

If he answered point-blank in this particular second, he would say no, which is why Noah wasn't going to answer it right away. "I love him. We both admitted that earlier tonight, and I believe him that he loves me. Until we came here, he never seemed to stray. It was only after Tara walked back into his life that things started to jump out as red flags." Noah said.

"They have always been really close. I can't deny that," Phillip admitted.

"Which I suppose is understandable. It doesn't excuse cheating on me, though," Noah said. It shouldn't. He felt that he deserved better. Noah wanted to believe that he did, at least.

There was a part of him that wanted to hurt Timothy right now. Phillip was sitting in bed next to him, and he wanted to kiss him just to make Timothy hurt. Yet, he wasn't going to do that. All that would do is hurt Phillip in the long run and potentially end a lifelong friendship. He had known Timothy for months. Phillip had known him his entire life. Noah sighed, "Do you mind if I just take a nap?" Phillip nodded.

* * *

When he woke up the next day, it was morning. He had turned off his phone the night before, knowing that he was bound to have a thousand texts, which is exactly what he woke up to. Timothy had texted him so many times his phone would not stop buzzing.

Noah was still upset. He thought that when he woke up that things would just automatically go back to how they were. He was, unfortunately, wrong. Timothy still had cheated on him. His heart was still broken, and yet he couldn't help but wonder if Timothy still loved him and if what he had said was actually true or just in the moment. Yet, if he had been lying, why lie, to spare Noah's feelings? He could have easily said that he just wasn't quite there yet with his feelings. Noah banged his head against the pillow.

The final text message poured in. It was from ten minutes ago. *Please tell me you are alright. I love you.* When he looked at the messages, more than half of them mentioned love. All this did was break Noah's heart further.

Phillip finally woke up. "Are you ok?" he asked. The two had slept in his bed together. Noah honestly had forgotten that he had fallen asleep. He never intended to spend the night. Yet, he also never intended to go back to Timothy's family home. He supposed he would have to. Noah guessed that he would have no choice. Timothy's parents would start to question things, and as angry as he was at Timothy, he wasn't going to have his parents start raising questions.

"I'm fine. I think I need to go back to Timothy's grandma's house." Noah honestly wanted to spend more time with Phillip. It was weird he wasn't sexually attracted to the boy in any way, shape, or form, but at the same time, he felt that in an alternate reality, they would have been best friends. Noah understood why Timothy was so fond of Phillip.

"Why don't you and I get some breakfast before we do. I don't want you going back angry and hungry at the same time," Phillip said with a smile.

Food was the last thing on Noah's mind right now, but he agreed.

* * *

The two boys ended up at a rather clean diner somewhere in town. Phillip made mention that this had always been a regular spot for himself with Collin and Timothy. Noah would bet big money that it also meant Tara, at least sometimes as well. He didn't care. He was ready for this entire week to be over, but of course, it was only Tuesday.

They had ordered, and then the front door opened. Noah honestly wasn't shocked that Phillip had called Timothy but even so. "Hi," his apparent boyfriend said.

Noah rolled his eyes and looked down, "Hi."

Phillip got up. "I'm going to go and make a call," he went outside.

"I know you hate me," Timothy said as he sat down. He just flat out said it.

"I don't hate you," Noah bluntly stated. He wanted to hate him. He should have hated him. Yet, he still loved him. "I love you," Noah said with anger in his voice. "I don't want to love you, but when you are really in love and not just infatuated, you just don't fall out of love."

Timothy nodded at this, "I really want things to work out between us. I wanted that experience to be with you. It was just very easy for me to fall back into things with Tara. I was with her practically my entire life in some way or another.

"You have to understand, you've seen my group of friends. It is practically non-existent. My first sexual experience with some guy who didn't care about me, and truth be told, I didn't care about him. It was just something to do." Noah wasn't really sure where he was going with this but hoped that Timothy would come up with a response that he could use.

The taller boy took a deep breath, "So, you don't think that sex means anything to you? I'm confused," Timothy admitted.

So was Noah if he was really honest. He had never had a fight with a boyfriend because he had never had a boyfriend. Many of the girls he would casually hang around got cheated on all the time, usually within their same friend circle. "Pretty much what I said earlier. I don't hate you. I just don't know if I want to be around you anymore." Noah said.

This clearly sunk Timothy's heart, "I suppose I figured that this was where things were going to go. I just don't know what to say or do. Like I said, the only other person I was ever with was Tara and the reason we broke up was that I was moving."

Which pretty much was the real icing on the cake.

Timothy clearly would still be with the girl if he hadn't moved. "Well, maybe you two can make long-distance work," Noah pointed out.

"I don't see a reality where that will happen. She said some really fucked up stuff after I came out to her last night," he explained.

So, he did come out to her. Noah had kind of forgotten that was the point of them going upstairs. "What could she possibly have said?" Noah asked, almost unamused. Timothy turned white. Whiter than he normally was, "What did she say?"

"She asked if she was going to catch something after what happened. Tara didn't say it out loud, but…"

It was pretty obvious what she was implying, "Tara is trash. Sorry to have to burst your bubble on that one. The fact that Collin, a straight guy, could understand your sexuality more than she could speaks volumes about her character. Then again, I suppose we aren't in bumfuck Kansas right now. So, maybe guys are more open to things like gay people around here, and maybe not all girls think of gay guys as play toys. Maybe."

Timothy buried his head into the table, "I do love you. Please know that."

Noah got up from the booth, "Yes, I know that, and I believe you one hundred and ten percent. I'm just not convinced that we can be together. I still need time. I'm sorry."

CHAPTER EIGHTEEN

TIMOTHY

Timothy spent the rest of Tuesday alone. Noah stayed out with Phillip most of the day, and Timothy sat in the attic room, staring at the wall. Tara had tried to text him a few times, saying she was sorry and that he was taking what she said out of context. Part of him wanted to believe that was true, but part of him knew that it didn't really matter. He and Tara were broken up, and he and Noah were in some weird gray area.

He didn't know what he could do or not do to fix things. Timothy loved Noah. It was the most natural thing in the world for him to say. "I'm in love with Noah Peters…, Noah and Timothy Peters, Timothy and Noah Powel." They might have been seventeen years old, but he already knew what the end game was for them. At least he thought he had known.

There was a knock at the door. "Come in," Timothy said. It was his father Leo. "Yes?" Timothy asked, confused.

"I was just wondering if you were still home. Where is Noah?" Leo asked.

"Um… Just taking a walk with Phillip," he explained. Timothy assumed that it could be the truth.

Leo nodded and went to sit at the edge of the bed, "So, are you enjoying being back home?"

Timothy didn't know. It felt good to be in misery, where he knew everyone. Those first few weeks in Kansas before Noah, it was just dreadful.

He didn't want to leave the house for anything unless he really had to, "It's been nice, I suppose."

His father gave him this weird look, "You and Noah are pretty close friends. This is going to be hard for me to ask you…"

Was his father really about to ask him if he was dating Noah? This wasn't a great time, "What do you mean?" Timothy stuttered to get out.

"Kansas was a concept that made sense in our heads. Well, my head, and I see how happy your mother has been here. I know how miserable she was in Kansas. The job was only supposed to last a year anyway. Since the house is no longer being rented, I think your mother and you should move back in. I'll stay at the house in Kansas until the end of next August. You enjoy your senior year with those boys and Tara," Leo explained.

It was as if his father was throwing a bag of bricks on his back. Leave Kansas right now? He couldn't do that. Could he? This could be what he needed and yet no at the same time. It wasn't as if he could take Noah with him. This was the worst possible time for something that would have been good news otherwise, "What if I wanted to stay in Kansas?"

Leo looked at him, confused, "You want to stay there?"

"I don't know. I mean, Phillip and Collin will always be my friends. I've realized that with being away from them. I love having Noah in my life, though, and I don't want to lose contact with him," Timothy curled up in a little ball in the bed.

"I just want you and your mother to be happy. Why don't you think about it for a few days? I'd rather not have your mother away from both of us, but I also know she really isn't adapting to the Kansas lifestyle," Leo explained. He patted his son on the shoulder and got up and left.

This was exactly what he needed, right. A choice between the life that he had always known and the life he wanted. If only the two worlds could bleed together. They would in a year but not if he left right now. No, if he left his new world, then it would be the death of his relationship with Noah. Noah couldn't know this, though. Could he? Timothy already knew what the blond boy would say if he were to inform him of this news. It would be to go back here, and then he would act all passive aggressive. Regardless if Noah was pissed off at him. He knew that Noah wanted what was best for Timothy. Which, in his mind, clearly meant being around his loved ones.

The tall boy started laughing. He laughed so hard that he fell to his side. If anyone were to see what he looked like right now, they might think he was having a nervous breakdown. Was he having a nervous breakdown? Probably. He would deal with that later.

So, many life-altering things had happened since he left Connecticut. Upon returning, only more crazy things had happened.

The door opened, and it was Noah. Timothy sat up in the bed. Noah came and sat down on the edge. "I love you," he said.

Timothy's heart sank, "I love you too and..." Noah put his hand on Timothy's lips.

"I love you, and I just want this craziness to be over with. I'm willing to reboot our relationship today once we get back to Kansas. You just have to promise me that it will never happen again. If, for whatever reason, you feel yourself falling for someone else, whether it be another guy or a woman, please just tell me, and we will figure things out from there." Noah looked Timothy in the eyes. "I guess there is a very tiny part of me that understands where you are coming from. I might not personally get it, but I suppose Phillip explaining things to me made it more real. You have some great friends."

Seriously, Timothy felt like he was about to start crying and laughing at the exact same time. His boyfriend was forgiving him but also Kansas. This was not happening right now. This couldn't seriously be a thing. "Yeah, I do have some great friends, but I have an even more incredible boyfriend," Timothy looked him in the eye.

"You really do. I blame the Kansas in me because I doubt I'd be ok with this if I was from anywhere else," Noah pointed as he crossed his arms.

It was obvious that Noah was slowly starting to return to his old lovable and quirky self, which was off-putting, considering what was going to happen. A large part of him wanted to just stay here forever, but Noah... "How many credits do you have left to complete?" Timothy asked him. Yes! Credits. If he had enough to graduate early, why wouldn't he?

Noah looked at him, a little confused. "This was totally the sexy conversation I expected to be having right now... Um, I'm four credits short of graduating technically. My English courses are actually college credited."

"So, you like it out here minus a few things, right?" Timothy asked.

"I mean, I like it better than I thought I would, that is for sure. Obviously, there are now certain people I hope that I never have to see again," Noah said with a face that said he meant it.

That was an understandable statement. "Do you think you could ever see yourself living here?" Timothy asked.

His boyfriend shrugged, "It's always a possibility. I've had my heart set on out West for so long now. My heart does belong to you even if it is still damaged."

Damn it. Not the words that Timothy needed to hear right now, "So, are we going to try going into the city for the parade?" It was best he just dropped that subject for another day. He was going to have no choice but to tell him before they left.

"I mean, so long as your ex isn't going, I'm down for spending more time with Phillip... and Collin too! They are both cool guys," Noah explained.

"You really seem to get along well with Phillip," Timothy said. It made sense. Phillip was just a really easy-going guy. Still, he would have guessed that Collin would have been the one he wanted to get to know better. Timothy had to admit to himself at least that Collin had been his first crush outside of Tara. He knew that Collin was straight, though, so it was more just an attraction than a full-blown crush.

His boyfriend started to turn a little white, which seemed odd. "Phillip's just a cool guy. We both have a lot in common. I suppose it makes sense that you would fall for me if you were friends with him."

"I guess..." Timothy still had no idea what he was talking about.

CHAPTER NINETEEN

NOAH

There was something about Phillip that Noah couldn't deny was charming. He couldn't put his finger on it, but there just was. He couldn't help but wonder if a small part was falling for him. Noah really didn't want to think about it, though, because he was with Timothy as much as he was pissed off at him, and he still was. He just knew that there was no use in being in an awkward position when it wasn't like he could easily go home.

Noah had checked the price of flights back to Kansas, but he didn't have enough. Even if he did, there would have been questions from Timothy's family. Noah wasn't going to accidentally out Timothy just because he was pissed off at him. What was he going to say? *Oh, we had a fight because we have been secretly dating, but I hooked up with Tara.* People didn't understand full-on gay people. They weren't about to understand the concept of bisexuality.

If he were honest, he did have to wonder what was taking Timothy so long to come out to his parents. They had dodged the subject of whether his parents were going to be upset with him or not. Noah had to assume that it was harder for parents to accept a son or daughter who was queer when they were an only child. He really doubted that Cheryl would have cared if he was gay if he was an only child. She was Cheryl, though. Plus, he wasn't an only child. He had Brick, who was already going to be a father. Plus, Kelly, who would more than likely be a mother one day. That said, Noah sort of wanted children. He had no idea if he would adopt or have a surrogate, though. They both had their positives and negatives in his mind. That was an active benefit of him being gay.

When he was actually ready for a child, it would be when he had one, not a second earlier, unlike his brother, who was about to be a father for the next eighteen to twenty-five years, depending on if he had any other children after this one. It almost felt like a trap. Brick was smarter than Amber or her family gave him credit for. It just pissed him off thinking about it. Though it did get Timothy's wandering around on him off his mind.

His boyfriend walked back into the attic room after having taken a shower. He hadn't dressed yet, which Noah had to admit was a positive, not a negative for him, "Fuck. You are so beautiful."

He got Timothy to blush. This was a rare treat because it just made him even sexier. "Stop, just because I'm naked doesn't mean I'm beautiful."

Noah started to stiffen in his groan. He got off the bed where he had been sitting and walked over to him. "You're beautiful with or without clothes on," as he kissed him on the lips. "Now get dressed so we can go about our day."

"You don't want to do or see more?" Timothy asked out loud as his chest was pounding.

"Nope," Noah said. He was going to be a tease for a while. It was one of the many ways that he would go about punishing Timothy. There were going to be many more serious repercussions, obviously. It was hard to act on them when he found the boy so hot, "Basketball season starts up right when we get home, right?"

Something clearly caught the tallboy off guard, "Um… Yeah. I think so."

It was going to be very hard to stay mad at him. Basketball uniforms were his weakness, "I can't wait to see you in your uniform."

"Oh, who knows what the future will hold," his boyfriend stated.

"What do you mean by that?" Noah asked, taken aback.

The curly-haired boy shrugged as he put a shirt on, "Nothing… I don't know."

Part of him wanted to ask what was wrong, but the other part of him wasn't so sure that he should right now. Being pissed off and in love was a difficult task, "Level with me... What's wrong, Timothy. It's better you tell me now than later. You should grasp that by now."

Timothy still wasn't wearing proper pants, but he stopped getting dressed. "Look... my dad told me something, and I don't know how to tell you without upsetting or making you choose. I can hardly choose myself."

Noah started to get a bit of a headache. "Ok. What did he tell you?"

"Apparently, my mom is tired of Kansas. Since the house isn't being rented out here anymore, she is moving back," Timothy explained.

"Are your parents separating?" Noah assumed that was what was going on.

This clearly took Timothy back a bit. "What? No, I mean, my dad obviously has to go back to Kansas for the rest of the contract, but she will move back into the house. Then he will be back next August."

Noah tried to figure out what this meant. Then it hit him. "Your parents want you to move back here, don't they?"

Timothy nodded, "Yeah, they do." Noah started to turn very pale. "I just want you to know that I'm in-different towards moving back or staying in Kansas. The issue is you, Noah, I'm in love with you. Phillip and Collin will always be my friends. My life here will always be waiting for me if and when I'm ready. The question is, will you be part of it anymore?"

Why was the world testing him? Noah went seventeen years without having anything spectacular or amazing happen to him. Yet now here he was with a boyfriend. Apparently, the universe wasn't going to just let that happen, though, so that boyfriend had to cheat on him. Then Noah fights back and says, *well, I can forgive him just this once.* So, what does the universe do?? This. "Are you going to be happy in Kansas for the rest of the year?" Noah asked?

"I'm going to be happy wherever you are. So long as I get to be part of that universe along with you," Timothy explained.

"You want to move back here after high school, though, right?" Noah asked.

The tall boy sighed, "I really don't want to move out West. I'm accustomed to the East coast. The West coast is a different world altogether."

Noah fell back on the bed, "Why can't life just be simple?"

Timothy walked over and sat next to him. "New York and Philadelphia are not that far from here if big city life is important to you. I'm not saying I'd never move out west. I'm just saying that right now, at this moment, I have no desire to make that move."

Noah sulked, "I mean, yes, the West Coast is important to me but in a vanity way. I can live anywhere so long as it isn't Kansas. Obviously, I do have to go back there for now."

"I mean, with four credits left, you could just stay here and go to school part time really, and even go to community college," Timothy pointed out.

"You've known about this for a few hours and you are already coming up with ideas for this to work?" Noah realized that it was a good thing but still felt awkward about it. He obviously didn't want to be separated from Timothy, but at the same time, he wondered if the distance would be a good thing for the moment. Noah wasn't going to say it out loud, though. Could he? He was still very much pissed off at Timothy, but love was overshadowing that anger, and now this. Why was this all becoming so overly complicated? All Noah wanted was a nice guy that he could fall for. Timothy was that on paper minus the cheating.

"I mean, you can think about it. I'm not telling you that you have to, obviously," Timothy pointed out.

Noah supposed that this was true. He could think about it. Unfortunately, he knew the answer that he was going to give him. He loved Timothy and knew that there was a universe in which they spend the rest of their lives together. He was hoping that it was the universe they currently lived in. He also knew that he was already planning on leaving his family at the end of the school year. It was looking like the East Coast might actually be that home right now instead of the West Coast. He just hoped that Timothy would be waiting for him when that happened.

PART THREE

CHAPTER TWENTY

TIMOTHY

Why was this call taking so long to load? It had been all of a day and a half since he had seen Noah's face. The boys had hugged for two and a half hours. It felt like before he was forced to get back on a plane for Connecticut. It was so weird to call him over the internet instead of texting him to pick him up so they could hang out in the park. He couldn't believe that he was on the verge of missing Kansas of all places. Kansas, but it was just Noah that he was missing. Kansas had been a horrid experience the more he discovered about himself as a person.

"Hey!" Noah said with a smile as the page finally loaded.

"Oh my gosh, hey!" Timothy said, very excited. He was getting nervous that the page wouldn't load. Sure, they could have just spoken on the phone, but it wasn't the same at all. "Ok, so still haven't unpacked at all aside from my computer. I'm planning on redoing my room entirely. My mom thinks that I should do some remodeling."

Noah smiled, "That could be a fun project."

"I don't know... I mean, yeah, I won't go away to school until next fall, but even so, it just seems weird for me to go about a project like that now," he explained. Timothy didn't mean to bring up college, but they were high school seniors. It was bound to be a regular conversation for the two boys. He just knew that Noah was still unsure of what he wanted for the fall.

The blond boy shuffled in his seat, "I mean, it will give you something to do. It sucks that you won't be able to be on the basketball team there this year."

He knew it did, but it wasn't like Timothy was going to be playing in college regardless. It was just stupid that the team captain clearly still hated him for something that had happened during middle school between them and, ironically, a girl. It wasn't Tara. "I'll survive. Plus, I can still go and see Phillip play."

"Say hi to Phillip for me! I mean, he texted me a few times yesterday but even so," Noah said with a smile.

Timothy was glad that Noah had taken a liking to his friends. It just meant that their bond was potentially sticking. They were still in a very awkward place, though. The two boys agreed that they would stay together. Timothy was happy about this. He wasn't going to give up Noah so easily.

"I've got to get going to work. I will text you later tonight!" Noah said with a smile. He hung up the video call before Timothy could say goodbye. He was still being distant.

* * *

"Come on, your shot!" Phillip screamed at Timothy as he stared into nothing.

Timothy realized that they were doing something, "Sorry... I was just thinking about Noah." It was probably around fifty degrees out, and he wasn't even cold as it just wasn't something that was on his mind. "I fucked up so royally, didn't I?"

Phillip dropped the ball, "I don't know if I would say that... I mean, you could have gone about things differently, yeah..."

That was terrible advice, but Phillip was never known for amazing advice. If anything, he was known for bad jokes and being awkward, which made sense as to why he and Noah got along so well. "I can't believe I let Noah talk me into coming back home," Timothy said.

His best friend shrugged, "It was probably for the best. The two of you needed space. Noah forgiving you so quickly was bound to have consequences had you been around each other all the time. That kid misses you because of the distance."

That was actually great advice. It really did make sense. The two boys would definitely have been spending every minute together if he were back in Kansas, which would have been awkward as hell if he really was being honest. Noah was the type to drag something on. He had every right in this particular situation, which Timothy hated to admit.

It was such a double-edged sword to be back home. He had his friends, but that beautiful blond boy was so far away. He did wonder about the blonde girl that he used to be with, though. Timothy had to wonder if they were ever going to speak again. Thus far, they had not. They had run into one another once, and he quickly ran. According to Collin, she had reached out to him about talking things over. Timothy just wasn't ready. It was so disgusting that her response would be that. Yes, he should have been more honest with her.

"You're overthinking something. I can always tell when you are overthinking something," Phillip said as he bounced the ball up and down.

Why did Phillip have to be so observant? "Yeah... Just Tara."

"I saw her the other day. She asked if you were doing alright," he explained.

"I guess she said the same with Collin too. I'm just not interested in dealing with her right now," Timothy sighed.

His friend dropped the ball. "It's ok to be angry at her, and maybe you never will be close with her again, but it might not be a bad thing to try and make things up with her. I'm just saying."

"I guess so," Timothy admitted. He didn't agree but whatever.

CHAPTER TWENTY-ONE

NOAH

Work had been boring. A total of ten customers came in. Technically that was busier than usual but even still. Noah had gotten through the day. It was weird. Timothy was gone, and it was both a good and bad thing. The reason it was good was that he had hurt him so badly. The bad was that he still loved him very deeply. It was obvious the two boys were in completely different worlds, and it was evident since the day they had met. Sure, Timothy had been nothing but nice and was willing to do anything to make Noah happy. That might have been the issue at hand. Timothy was trying so desperately to reinvent himself but was still very much himself. It only became more obvious when they were in Connecticut.

Noah dropped his bookbag down on the ground of his room. Did he want to call Timothy and listen to him talk for an hour? Part of him thought yes. The other part of him knew he needed to study in order to escape Kansas in the fall. He needed to escape Kansas on his own. He always knew that was the way it was going to end. Was he running off to the West Coast? He was still applying to those schools. There was no reason not to. With his luck, he would apply to a bunch of schools on the East coast and not get into any of them anyway, and he wasn't sure if that was considered good or bad luck at this point.

There was a knock at the door. "Can we talk?" Brick asked his brother.

Noah turned around, "Yeah. Totally." He gestured for him to sit on the bed.

"Amber just admitted that she has been cheating on me," Brick explained.

This was not the conversation that Noah thought they would be having. "What the hell? With whom?" Noah asked.

Brick laid back in the bed, "I have no idea. Apparently, there have been multiple guys, and it has been going on since before graduation."

It took Noah a moment to process this. "Wait, does this mean?"

His older brother sat back up, "Yes. Well, actually, I don't know what it means yet, but yes. There is a chance that this child will not turn out to be mine. I told her we are getting a DNA test tomorrow. I looked into it. You can actually do it before the child is born."

This couldn't be happening. Noah couldn't tell his brother that he was secretly hoping that the kid turned out not to be his. "I mean, this could change everything," Noah said.

"Obviously, I broke up with her. I could just tell something was off. I just didn't want to admit to it. It would be one thing if it was a one-time thing. We could potentially work through it. Multiple guys, though? What the hell is wrong with her? If the child is mine, I will obviously take care of it but not with her. I'll make sure her smug parents know why too," Brick looked both furious and relieved.

It seemed that neither brother needed to admit it out loud, but they both sort of already knew the truth. The child was more than likely, not going to turn out to be Brick's. "So, what happens when it turns out not to be your kid?" Noah asked.

"I think I'll get the hell away from here for a while. I mean, I've been saving money for when the baby was born for an apartment and stuff," Brick explained.

"Get out of Kansas," Noah said loudly.

His brother gave him a weird look, "Why?"

"Look at everyone you graduated with. Half of them are already engaged, and the other half have kids on the way themselves. You graduated last May, for crying out loud! You might not end up with Amber, but if not her, it will just be some other girl you graduated with or some girl who went to a different high school in the next town. Mom will understand. I'm leaving the moment I graduate or in the Fall too," Noah finally admitted to his brother.

"It seems like you have already thought this out for yourself," Brick pointed out.

Noah had never really thought to tell his family of the whole plan. They knew he was looking into the West Coast, but clearly, no one took him seriously. Everyone talked about going out of state. No one really did. "I need to try," Noah said.

Brick nodded in understanding, "I don't know if I'm going to leave Kansas permanently, but maybe I'll go out East for a little bit and do some sightseeing. I've always wanted to check out some of the big cities. So, how is Timothy doing? Have you guys spoken yet today?"

"I guess I should tell you since you just told me about Amber. When we were in Connecticut, Timothy cheated on me," Noah admitted.

"Wait. What? With whom?" Brick asked.

This was a story he really didn't feel like reiterating. "Timothy is apparently bisexual, which doesn't bother me. I'm the first guy that he has ever dated. He dated a girl named Tara for years back home. He went to tell her about him being bi, and instead, they slept together," Noah explained.

The older brother shook his head in disbelief, "I thought he was a better person than that to cheat on you."

Noah didn't really think that Timothy was a bad person. He just thought that Timothy was confused and got caught up in the moment. It didn't change the fact that he was still pissed off at him. "We are still technically together, but obviously, we aren't anywhere near one another. He wanted me just to go and finish the school year with him up there."

"I mean, the distance is probably a good thing. You can decide what you want better when you aren't around him," Brick explained.

This was what Noah thought too. It was just hard not to miss Timothy, which was potentially a sign that he wanted to be with him still. Yet, he really wasn't sure. This was getting very annoying to think about. Noah wondered if what was best is that he just didn't think about it at all?

CHAPTER TWENTY-TWO

TIMOTHY

Phillip had to get home to study, but Timothy wasn't ready to go home even if it was already getting dark out. His mother didn't care so long as he kept the tracking device on his phone activated. He just wasn't interested in going home. He knew that Noah was avoiding him at all costs, which was understandable. It just made Timothy even more miserable and distraught than he already was. All the boy wanted was for his boyfriend to forgive him. He had to wonder if that really was just too much to ask.

As Timothy continued to kill time, a very familiar but now unwanted face popped out from around the corner. "Timmy, what are you doing here so late?" Tara asked, both shocked and concerned to see him.

"I'm just wandering around. I need to get going," he explained to her.

Tara chased after him, "Wait, please, we need to talk about a lot of things."

Timothy turned back around. "I don't need you to berate me or call me a disgrace or whatever."

His former girlfriend frowned, "Look, I'm sorry for asking you what I did. You just threw me off entirely, and I guess something randomly just popped into my head. It wasn't right, and I know it wasn't right."

It was so easy to want to forgive his former girlfriend. It just wasn't the right time to do so. "Look, I guess I'll thank you for saying sorry, but I'm not sure what to tell you. What you said was really fucked up. Plus, what we did, and that is all on me, really fucked up my relationship with Noah."

"You guys broke up, right?" she asked.

A chill came over him. "What do you mean, broke up? Why would we have broken up?" Timothy screamed at her.

Tara jumped back a little, "I mean, I just assumed since you moved back, which I'm happy about at least for Phillip and Collin's sake. They missed you. I missed you."

He missed them, and he missed her. Timothy wasn't in love with her. The boy was in love with Noah Peters. Tara was now a part of his past, a part of his past that he had cherished. He had cherished her. She had always been there for him growing up. They shared so many firsts together, which included the first time they had sex. At least he assumed it was Tara's first time. Why on earth did he care?

"I'd like to meet Noah the next time he comes to town. Clear the air with him," she sounded so nervous.

Would there be a next time at this point? He sure as hell hoped that there would be. Timothy longed for the nights in which he and Noah would hold each other in the backseat of Noah's car. Those were the days. It had been so brief and yet so damn powerful.

The curly-haired boy looked at his ex, "I'm sure that in an alternate universe, the two of you would have been best friends the moment you met one another." Timothy thought about Noah's friends back in Kansas. Lord, aside from Brick and maybe his boss Sasha there weren't many people for Noah to confide in. The last thing he needed to do was keep this all in his mind. "He is just one of those very lovable people. Noah is sort of anxious, but in the most adorable way ever."

The blonde girl frowned, "You really do love him? You never seemed to gush about me."

Timothy walked a little closer to her, "I mean look. I loved.... I love you, Tara, even if I think what you said was beyond fucked up. You were always a great friend. I think it made sense that the two of us dated at one point. We were just always together. Do I think in an alternate universe we would have ended up married sometime after high school? Yes. Do I think we would have been happy? Yes, but I would still be bisexual."

Bisexuality was such a weird concept for people to understand. Timothy didn't even think that Noah understood it. He really was bisexual, though. As madly in love with Noah as he was, there was a large part of him that was still very turned on by Tara. He had always admired men from afar as well as other women. Timothy just wished that he had not cheated on Noah with a woman. It felt like he was just embracing a terrible stereotype of bisexuals that he didn't intend to become part of. It was a heat of the moment situation.

CHAPTER TWENTY-THREE

NOAH

It wasn't that Noah was a prude. He just could have lived without hearing Lily discuss her sex life. Oh, how was he friends with this girl? Timothy had been right. Lily was kind of a loser. Well, no, not kind of a loser, she was a loser. This was a girl who would probably work at the store with his mother after dropping out of community college and then get knocked up by Ned. Lord, was it disturbing to think about Lily and Ned getting it on. Yet he really didn't need to imagine. Lily had shared their sex tape once. It was Ned's birthday present last year. This was his closest and oldest friend.

The bell rang, "Oh darn... I need to get to the counseling office." This day had not even started, and yet he was ready for it to be over with. Brick was supposed to get the DNA test results back today. The family had already obviously said they would support him regardless. Aside from Kelly, though, no one was really hoping the child would be his. Amber's family wanted to sue for defamation. It wasn't as if they had been running around, screaming that Amber was loose. Noah suspected that they were just that kind of lawsuit-happy.

"I'll tell you more about it at lunch!" Lily explained as Noah ran down the hall.

Clearly, Noah was going to have lunch off campus today. That was a given.

The blond boy walked into the counseling office. Mrs. Barker was standing in the entrance, reading a file, "Noah, you are late!"

Noah looked at his watch. "I'm late by like half a minute," he said with a look of confusion.

"No excuses," she explained.

He looked around. Amy and Luna were not here yet themselves. "So, when Amy and Luna finally show up at the end of the period, will you be berating them as well?" Noah asked.

Mrs. Barker looked him right in the eye, "Those two are late because they are studying."

"You know this how? I legit know they are in the parking lot either smoking or drinking or some shit like that," Noah told his instructor. He wasn't putting up with her bullshit today.

She looked at him and seemed to twitch, "So, you are late, and you use foul language? I'm really considering detention or suspension."

"I'm really considering reporting you to the district or the state or whatever. You have had it out for me since Freshman year. I'm gay. Get the fuck over it," Noah walked past her and sat down at a table.

The crazy middle-aged woman walked over and slammed whatever she was reading down, "How dare you use foul words around me."

"How dare you think that I will put up with you any longer," Noah had no idea what had gotten into him today. Was it the revelation that Brick probably wasn't a father? The fact that Lily had just spent twenty minutes discussing her creepy sex life. Or the fact that he was still beyond pissed at Timothy but missed him to death. "You have two options as far as I'm concerned. Go sit in your office and wait for your first appointment, or we spend all day with the principal together. Now we both know he will side with you. I'm not stupid. That said, when I figure out a way to get the local news involved, there might be a few more complaints. I leave at the end of the year. You have another twenty, possibly thirty years at this hell hole?" He laughed, "Go sit down."

There was about a minute of silence between them, but then Mrs. Barker's first appointment came in. She walked into her office with the girl and did not come out when the student left.

* * *

As he had promised himself, Noah had lunch off campus, which was technically not allowed, but he didn't give a damn. Noah had spent years following the rules of society. It got him a short-term boyfriend at seventeen years old. Well, he supposed that they were still together. They were together. Yes, he and Timothy were together. He highly doubted that Timothy would answer his phone right now, but he needed to talk with him.

It took a minute, but Timothy answered the video call. "Hey," he said. It looked like he was outside somewhere himself.

Noah smiled, "Hey," was all Noah could say himself.

"Are you alright? Isn't it lunchtime there?" Timothy asked.

"I couldn't sit with Lily today. I don't know what happened, but I think it was the last straw today. I can't really explain it. Lily is an idiot. Mrs. Barker can go to hell, and she probably will. Brick is going to be leaving the state soon for some traveling. I still love you. I love you," Noah admitted. This was where it was hard, though, "I love you, but I don't think that the two of us are meant for one another."

Timothy looked as if his heart just broke into two, "What are you saying?"

Noah sighed, "I've spent the last seventeen years, allowing myself to just exist. In this Godforsaken place, coming out was the world's way of saying, ok, but that is all we are giving you. I love you. It's so hard not to be around you every minute of the day, but I need to do something for myself. I need to go out West after high school."

His boyfriend just sat on the other end of the call quietly, "I mean, why don't you take some time to figure out what out West means? I support you regardless, though." Timothy hung up the phone. He hung up without saying anything else.

It was obvious that Noah had just hurt the boy. He knew that he technically should feel bad, but for once, he didn't. Timothy had cheated on him, and in hindsight, he had allowed it out of fear of losing him. He now realized that it was better to have loved and been loved than never at all. Noah had just had his first love and was able to accomplish it in Kansas of all places. This era and day especially would go down as a fond memory.

He might never speak with Lily after high school. His mother and siblings might have to visit him instead of the other way around. It didn't really seem to matter anymore. Noah was done being compliant with a backward town in a backward state smack dab in the middle of the country.

CHAPTER TWENTY-FOUR

TIMOTHY

The rest of the school day consisted of him just looking at Noah's photo on his phone. No one seemed to notice around him. He walked out of school, and Collin ran over. He was supposed to drive him home before basketball practice. Timothy finally looked up at his phone, "We broke up."

"What?" Collin asked in total shock.

The tall boy sighed, "I deserve it. I broke his heart and then ran." That's the reality. He could have forced himself to stay in Kansas for the rest of the year. His mother might have been lonely back here, but he could have stayed in Kansas and fixed things. Timothy ran. He admitted it even if only to himself and Collin now. "I fucked up so badly."

Collin sadly nodded, "What are you going to do about it?"

What would Timothy do about it? This was a good question. "I think I just need to give up?"

His best friend looked him in the eye, "I'm sorry, what now? You have never been one to give up."

That was true. In his life, Timothy never gave up on anything. Yet, this time was different. "Noah made it clear. He doesn't think that we make sense together. So, I suppose it is time to move on. I don't really want to live in California, even for college. I'm an East Coast guy born and raised. I get it. He is from the middle of the country. He wants something bigger.

I just don't understand why he can't live out that fantasy in New York or Philadelphia or Boston even."

"I mean, the North East can be a bit conservative itself. I could see him wanting to live out his best life on the West Coast," Collin pointed out.

Timothy supposed that made sense. Phillip walked over as he was lost in thought. "What's going on?" he said.

Collin looked at him with a look that said they needed to do damage control. "Noah broke up with him."

Phillip's jaw dropped. "Wait. What? How? I thought the two of you were in a better place!" Phillip seemed more invested than he probably should have been.

"He wants different things than I do. Plus, I did hurt him. I can't just go around denying that." He saw Tara from a distance, "I also hurt her."

"Yeah, but she said some really horrible things in return," Phillip pointed out.

If he had to be honest, he was starting to forgive Tara. It might not have been the best time to admit that, but it was the truth. Timothy had no idea if they would ever call themselves friends again, though. "How on earth did my life get so dramatic? I swear it's like we are living on one of my grandma's soap operas."

"Oh yeah, because your life is that exciting," Phillip playfully joked with him.

Ok, so maybe he wasn't a mobster's son or the son of a car mogul like on a soap opera. He needed to get out of his head. "We need to do something fun," Timothy said.

"I have a basketball." Collin pointed out.

"I'm down," Phillip said.

Timothy grabbed his friend's hand and marched off. "We will see you later!" Timothy screamed back at Collin.

Phillip looked at him, "So, what are we going to do?"

"I have no idea but something fun." He looked at Tara, who guiltily frowned at him. He looked away, "Something fun."

* * *

The two boys ended up back in his bedroom. They got someone to buy them liquor. "Ok... Drinking. That should be fun, right?" Timothy asked.

His friend looked at him from across the bed. "This might not be the best idea considering the fact that you are trying to get over a breakup."

"Oh, come on." He took a swig of the vodka. It was the most disgusting thing he had ever drank. He would sip on wine or beer sometimes, but that was about it. Timothy didn't even like the taste of those. The tall boy just thought that if it was clear as water, it wouldn't have a taste to it. "What is this - cleaning supplies?" as he threw the bottle at Phillip.

"I think we should talk about something instead of drinking away our sorrows," Phillip tried to insist.

Timothy laughed as he laid back on the bed, "What could you possibly be in sorrow about? Your life is perfect. Mine is the one in shambles."

Phillip took a quick swig of the vodka, "Jesus Christ. What is this bottom shelf shit? Regardless, my life is not perfect." Phillip looked directly into Timothy's eyes.

"I beg to differ. I bet that Noah probably texts you before he texts me, which I don't even care, but I don't know where that friendship even came from," Timothy explained.

"We just sort of bonded over the fact that we are both... gay," Phillip chose to blurt out.

The tall friend shot back up in bed, "I'm sorry, what now?"

His friend nodded, "I'm gay, Timothy."

This was not something that Timothy expected to happen ever. He would never have thought in a million years that Collin or Phillip would be gay. "Wow... I mean, I'm happy for you and honored you can tell me about it. I just never would have guessed."

"My plan was actually to tell you about it when you came home for Thanksgiving. Then we found out about you and Noah. Noah actually told me right before you did," Phillip explained.

It all sort of made sense as to why Phillip, of all people, would bond with Noah. It wasn't that they made no sense having a bond together. It was just the fact that Noah was such an introvert and Phillip and extrovert.

Plus, Phillip was kind of an idiot. A lovable idiot but yeah, "Do you like Noah?" Timothy blurted himself. He didn't actually mean to say that out loud.

"I mean, in an alternate universe, I suppose we could have been more than friends. He belongs with you, though," Phillip explained.

Did Noah belong with Timothy? That was a question. Timothy glanced over at his dresser and got up. On top of it was a stack of papers, which shocked Timothy to see. It was Noah's manuscript. He had totally forgotten about this, "I never got around to reading this."

"What is it?" Phillip asked.

Timothy looked at Phillip, "A book that Noah wrote or a story or something. I mean, I probably should throw it out. It's just going to make me think of him, but maybe I should take a short glance or something?"

His friend nodded, "I think you should do more than that. If anything, it might give you closure. If it is really bad, then you can laugh and realize you dodged a bullet. If it is really good, then maybe you will continue to wallow for months on end. Regardless you have a new goal!"

This was the Phillip that Timothy knew and loved, "I suppose I will give it a try. I mean, you are right." The only issue that Timothy had to face now was finding out how talented Noah really was. He spent several months with the blond boy. There was no doubt that he was going to be a genius with his writing.

CHAPTER TWENTY-FIVE

NOAH

"I'm thinking of closing up early tonight. What do you think?" Sasha asked Noah.

The blond boy was looking at his phone. He had been on the register for the last half-hour. Noah realized that Sasha had been talking, "Oh um... Sounds good."

"You never should have broken up with that boy. It's obvious that you are head over heels in love with him," Sasha pointed out.

She just didn't understand. No one did. "I want to live out West after high school. He doesn't want to leave the East coast. It just didn't work."

Sasha rolled her eyes, "Oh, you silly young homosexual. Do you know why I stay in Wichita of all places?"

"I don't know... You enjoy being a big fish in a small pound?" Noah just assumed that was the situation.

His boss nodded, "Yes, and no. Noah Peters, the world is full of idiots no matter where you go. San Francisco might be the gayest place you can think of, but there are gay people all over. Plus, you don't want to live around gay people. You want to live around people."

That made absolutely no sense. "Is there a difference?" Noah asked.

Sasha sat down on an armchair, "Queer life is amazing. Drag, art, passion, so on and so forth. It is all fun and games, but you can get that substance anywhere. We have drag here. We have gay bars. You can live ridiculously cheap if you so wish."

"That sounds nice, and all in theory, but it isn't the same as experiencing it," Noah pointed out.

She stood back up, "Sweetheart, unless you intend to try and become an actor, why the hell would you go out West? New York is a kitty-corner away from Connecticut. There is gay life surrounded all around you out there. California is a different beast entirely. Plus, really, no snow on Christmas? Really?"

All this conversation was making him realize was that Sasha made no sense in Kansas. "I mean, maybe you are right," he had to admit that he was just looking for excuses to stay away from Timothy at this point. He was still upset with him. He got a text from Brick. "Oh boy… I need to get going!" He grabbed his coat.

"Remember what I just told you! Let it sink in!" Sasha screamed.

* * *

Noah ran into his house and into the living room. "You have the test results?" he blurted out.

His brother held the envelope while his mom and Kelly sat across from him. "I don't know if I want to open it." Brick said.

"Let me do it for you. I want to be the one to personally go demand all the money back that you spent on that girl," Cheryl stated.

It was obvious at this point they were all eager to hear the news. Brick took a deep breath and opened the envelope. "Holy shit," he said as he dropped the paper down.

Noah picked the paper up. He thought he would be happy with the results, and yet he wasn't. "I'm sorry Brick. I'm really sorry."

Cheryl stood up and started dancing, "I'm not a grandmother!"

"Does this mean I'm not an aunt?" Kelly asked obnoxiously.

"What the hell do you think it means?" Noah asked her.

Brick took the paper back from Noah, "I just can't believe this is the truth. Yet I do, unfortunately."

When Noah first found out that the baby would more than likely not be Brick's, he was so happy. Yet now he just felt bad for his brother. He knew that Brick was ready to be a father because he had just spent nine months prepping to be one. "I mean do we celebrate or grieve?" Noah finally said out loud.

His mother clearly got the hint because she finally stopped dancing. She sat next to her eldest child, "I'm glad we are finding this out now and not eighteen years later. Does she even know who the actual father is?"

Brick shook his head no, "I don't think so. I mean, if she does, then she isn't telling me. I highly doubt that any of the guys she might have potentially been with are going to step up."

No more Amber in their lives. This was a relief. Yet, no more Timothy. That was a different situation altogether. He ducked out of the living room and went down the hall to his bedroom. He got out his phone went to call Timothy. He had his hand on the screen about to hit call, but he just couldn't do it. It was hard to break up with someone that you knew you potentially would never see or hear from again. Sure, they had social media to look at, but never again would he probably speak with Timothy Powell. The first boy he had ever loved. The first boy that had ever loved him. Some people needed to have multiple loves in their life. Timothy obviously had loved another at one point. Yet, for Noah, he was now having trouble imagining what a life without Timothy was going to look like.

He thought about Timothy's warm lips as they pressed up against his own. Noah thought of wrapping his arms around Timothy's thin body. The smell of Timothy's overpriced but very sensual cologne. This was all starting to hit him. There was a knock at the door. It was Brick. "Hey," Noah said.

"Are you doing alright?" Brick asked.

"I officially broke up with Timothy, and I officially regret it a hundred and ten percent." Noah's head fell on to his pillow, "What did I do?"

Brick sat down on his bed, "Something you clearly regret. Noah, you don't need to live in California. You've never lived in California. You could be miserable there for all you know."

"Yeah, but I won't know until I actually live there," Noah pointed out.

His brother rolled his eyes, "You said to me the other day. What is left in Kansas? Nothing. I'm just going to add the fact that you don't know what you are going to find somewhere else. That goes for anywhere you go."

He knew that Brick was trying to go somewhere with this conversation, but he couldn't figure it out. "So, where are you heading to yourself exactly?"

"I'm probably going to go out to Boston, actually. I've always wanted to see the landmarks, if I'm honest. Then I'm going to look into a few colleges in Illinois when I get back. It normally takes people an extra semester or two to graduate college, so I can start up now and still finish up around twenty-three hopefully," Brick admitted.

Clearly, his brother had already realized that this kid wasn't his. He wouldn't be this prepared if he didn't think otherwise. "Well, two college-educated Peters children. Kelly is going to have no choice but to go now."

"Honestly, I think one of us might need to take Kelly with us wherever we go. It might be the only way to yank her out of this place," Brick said out loud.

It was sadly the honest truth, but Noah didn't want to have to say it himself.

CHAPTER TWENTY-SIX

TIMOTHY

Phillip had left five hours ago. It took him the entire five hours to read the entirety of the story that Noah had written. It was official. Timothy was going to miss Noah for the rest of his life. The way that this boy wrote was just so moving. It was so different than anything he had ever read in his life. It was like reading something he shouldn't be reading but never wanting to put it down. It was so hard to explain.

There was a knock on the door. It was his mother, "Are you alright? Dinner will be done soon."

"Yeah… I'm fine." He was actually a little bit drunk from the vodka still.

Ana looked at her son, "I know you aren't right. I can always tell when something is wrong."

"I broke up with my boyfriend," Timothy said. It took him a minute to grasp what he just told his mother. "I mean," he sat up in his bed. He didn't know what to say. His mother walked further into the room and over to him. She just hugged him, "You're gay?"

Timothy wasn't expecting to be hugged by his mother when he came out. He really never knew what he was expecting, "I mean…"

"I never was a fan of that Tara. Jewish or no, she was not the person for you," Ana admitted out loud.

That confirmed a few theories that Timothy had over the years, "I'm actually bisexual."

Ana sat down next to him, "Still, Tara is not the person for you."

Well, he already knew that, "Ok… Great. I was dating Noah, though. You know from Kansas."

She brushed her hair back, "Well, he wasn't a Jew either. I did like him, though. At least in comparison with Tara. I sort of figured he was gay."

"Did you think I was gay?" Timothy decided to ask. It was a valid question to ask.

"I never really cared about what you were so long as you were happy. Your father was a different story. He suspected," Ana explained.

That made too much sense and kind of hurt Timothy to find out, "Well… We broke up, and I'm heartbroken."

She continued to hug him. Potentially a little too tight, "Well, if it is because of the distance, you can always move back with your father. I'm going to be going back to the old law firm at the end of the month. This domestic thing was fun for a few weeks but got old quickly."

"It is because of distance but not the distance of Connecticut to Kansas but Connecticut to California. He wants to move out West," Timothy explained.

She shook her head, "Who on earth would want to live out West? It's hot, no snow, too much sunlight. No. No, never."

His mother was not helping as much as it seemed like she was trying to be supportive; it just wasn't helping. This was just so typical of how she acted around him. Timothy thought for a moment. The tall boy never really thought of how he would come out to his parents or if he ever would. Noah was the reason why he wanted to come out. It just felt so weird to have to say *I'm bisexual* to his parents or anyone for that matter.

People understood what gay meant. People understood what straight meant. It was everything in between those two things that people tended to take issue with. It seemed that his mother didn't care. She clearly would have preferred he be with someone Jewish that wasn't Tara. However, she did seem to like Noah. Clearly, that did not matter anymore. Noah was no longer going to be in his life.

"I'm going to call your father. We can arrange tickets for you to go and be with him for the rest of the semester," Ana explained, getting out her phone.

Timothy jumped out of his bed, "Wait! No! I told you, Noah and I broke up. There were other reasons involved, mom. I can't just go back there now. It would be very awkward."

She gave him a very unpleasant look, "Timothy Powell. I will not have you sitting around this house miserable for the next few months before graduation. We can either fix this now, or I will be signing you up for every after-school activity under the sun."

Lord, she loved to be difficult, "Can we just give it a day or so for me to figure out how I want to handle this?"

"I suppose. We should probably tell your father about your sexuality," Ana explained.

Did they really have to? Timothy supposed they did. At this point, with his mother knowing it wasn't that big a deal. Timothy would never be close to his father, but he didn't think either of them would ever hate each other. "Can you just do it by yourself?" Timothy asked.

His mother looked at him again, but this time confused, "I suppose I can. I'm sure he will want to discuss it with you at some point, though. He loves you, Timothy. We both do. I want you to always know that." She gave him a kiss on the forehead, "Oh shit! I left the oven on. I need to rescue that brisket!"

The tall boy walked over to the mirror on his wall. He looked into it. This was his life now, and there was such a weight lifted off his shoulder, but another one still stood. There had to be a way to get over him. There just had to be.

His phone wrang. It was Noah. Timothy didn't even hesitate. "Hey," he said into the camera.

"I love you," Noah smiled.

"I just came out to my mom. Phillip came out to me earlier, too, by the way. Thanks for being there for him when he told you. Oh, I love you too." He really did. He loved him more than life itself at this point. "So, why are you calling?"

Noah took a moment to respond. It was apparent he had no idea what to say, "Maybe I don't need the West Coast."

Timothy nodded, "Well, you don't need it, but if you want it, you should go for it."

"Yes, but my reasons for the West Coast were because I had no idea what I wanted in life. I do now. I know exactly what I want. I want you, Timothy Powel," Noah admitted.

This was all so overwhelming, but everything that Timothy needed right now. "I need you, Noah Peters. I need you all day, every day. Why did I move back? My mom just told me I could move back and be with you."

Noah's face shot up with excitement, but then he shook his head, "No. I want you to stay there. Trust me. It is for the best. Your friends and family are there. All I have going for me here is family. Who I love and will miss, but Brick is already on his way to Boston for some site seeing. You made a great point. I can graduate at the beginning of January, technically. I have some money saved up. My mom and I still need to talk but, Timothy, can I come to stay with you and you mom?" he giggled.

"I can't imagine she would say no. It might help a little bit though, if you pretend you are converting," Timothy joked.

Clearly, this went over Noah's head. "I'll look into that... I have to wonder what the future holds for us?"

"I imagine that whatever it holds for us, it will be rather brilliant," Timothy smiled.

NINE MONTHS LATER...

"Yes. We will be fine. I promise you we will be fine," Timothy told his mother." His father stood next to her and had a slight smile on his face. Timothy still wasn't close with his father in the slightest, but it seemed as though they were finally starting to get to know one another. Maybe the distance of a few miles with college would change everything?

"I need you to make sure that Noah is in bed at a decent hour. Do not let him get into his head. Oh, you already know this already. I'm texting both of you daily to make sure you are fine," Cheryl told Timothy and Noah. She had driven up with Kelly in order to see the two boys off at school.

Noah shook his head, "Mom... I'm going to be fine. I know how to handle being away from you. I've already been living away from home for the last few months."

The two boys sat in their tiny little New Haven apartment. Timothy was going off to university. Noah was still in community college. He just didn't want to spend the money. They both got into the same school. Noah was hoping to defer his offer. It was thanks to him mostly, though, that they were able to live off-campus technically. They had actually started renting it a month earlier but didn't move in until today. Noah spent the free time in-between the few college classes he took at Timothy's high school, working full-time hours, and saving every penny. Then, when they both graduated, Noah's psychedelic boss from Kansas sent a card in the mail with a couple of grand in cash. Noah tried sending it back three or four times, but each time she sent more. Apparently, she had sold the bookstore and was moving to Texas herself. Noah himself apparently had inspired her to be a small fish in a big pond. From her social media, she was already the queen of the Dallas scene, though.

The families talked a few more hours before they finally managed to get them to go back home and to their hotel for the night. They would have breakfast in the morning before Timothy started his first class, and Noah went to his class. "Ok... I thought they would never leave."

Noah laughed, "I mean, they want to make sure we will be ok. It's too bad that Brick couldn't have been here, though." Brick, his brother, was in Boston, and it wasn't that long of a drive away. He had only meant to stay a few weeks but ended up chatting it up with a contractor who worked there. He ended up deciding that he wanted to stay instead of going off to Chicago. Noah and Cheryl were a little annoyed that he wasn't in college, but supposedly he was making money. His apartment was rather nice. "I also kind of wish that my mom and Kelly would move up here. Then again, Kelly still isn't able to drive, and I'm not driving her to school in the mornings. They can stay in Kansas at least until she turns sixteen." The blond boy's phone went off, "Oh joy... Lily is pregnant and engaged. How on earth is she already rocking the mom jeans? She only graduated a few months ago. Damn."

Timothy laughed, "Are you going to congratulate her?"

His boyfriend looked up from his phone, "Oh... Um, maybe later. I also have an email that I need to read over." He walked into their bedroom.

CHAPTER TWENTY-SEVEN

NOAH

Things started out great. They became rocky as time went on, and then they healed as time continued further. Noah obviously had to interact with Tara once he moved up here. They sort of went to the same school. He didn't foresee the two of them being best friends, but he knew that Timothy and her would always be friends. Phillip mentioned with a frown a few months back that it was obvious the once close group had grown further apart after Timothy moved back. None of them seemed to be rather saddened by this.

Collin, in a bizarre turn of events, was going to school out west. He received a partial basketball scholarship at a school out there. As for Phillip, he was going to be going to school with Timothy. He lived in the dorms. Noah could definitely tell that he was dating someone, but Timothy was insistent that Phillip would have told him.

As for the blonde girl herself, Tara, she ended up going to school somewhere in Massachusetts. Timothy will text with her on occasion but not really.

It was weird to find out that Lily was pregnant. Noah kind of figured that she would end up barefoot and pregnant, but he had hoped that there was potentially a chance she would maybe at least graduate college first. Clearly, that was not going to be the case for her. She wasn't even the only girl who was knocked up. Apparently, both Amy and Luna from the counseling office were engaged, and one of them was rumored to be pregnant. It really didn't shock Noah at all. It had shocked him more when he had found out that Sasha finally decided to get the hell out of Dodge. He was so happy for her to finally be gone. She deserved more.

The blond boy sat down at his desk. Their new shared bedroom was half the size of Noah's room back in Kansas. He opened his email. It had gone off earlier, but he wanted to be able to give this message his all. He knew what it was, and he didn't want to spoil anything. Noah read over the message about five times over. Timothy walked in. Noah handed him his laptop, "Read this for me."

"Ok, fine, but can you go look at the TV? I swear my grandmother's soap opera is haunting me right now. The channel won't change, and it is flickering back and forth to the same scene, *Vivica will be back... Vivica will be back... Vivica will be back...* It sounds like some kind of creepy omen," Timothy explained. He sat down at his desk chair and looked over the message. Noah ran out into the living room, quickly fixing the TV from glitching. He ran back into their bedroom. Timothy was staring at him with the biggest smile ever, "Congratulations." He got up and hugged his boyfriend.

"Do you think it is too soon?" Noah asked. He wasn't sure if he was ready, but he took a whim and sent in the submission.

Timothy was clearly crying into Noah's shoulder, "I think it was the perfect time. You deserve this so much."

At the beginning of the summer, he had submitted his manuscript to about fifty or so different book agents. One of them finally responded today. As of today, Noah Peters was going to be represented and on his way to a book deal. "This is just everything."

His boyfriend looked at him, "Is it everything you always wanted?"

"No," Noah smiled, "I got that the day I met you."

The two boys looked at one another for a very long minute. They both were saying it without saying it. They were in love and ready to spend the rest of their lives together. They kissed. The kiss would go on for a while before turning into something much more.

ACKLNOWLEDGEMENTS

First and foremost, my friend and business partner Nikki Baker. We met one another in the Youtube comment section of some Broadway musical clip over ten years ago. I was living in Kansas at the time. We plotted against the world in order to forge our careers as we switched from wannabe actors to actual writers.

My artist Luviiilove… You just manage to knock it out of the park time after time. We both know I wasn't originally going to have you do the cover for this book. I wanted to distinguish the difference between, *Between Heaven and Hell* and this novel. Then I realized that interviewing and testing out new artists is annoying especially when I know you always deliver at 250% capacity. I came to you asking for a "simple" looking cover and you knocked it out of the park big time! The moment I saw this cover was the moment my confidence in not only this book but for all of the upcoming year (2021) would be in mega drive. Get ready because we have several projects to prep for!

Thank you to Josh Patterson for forcing me to believe in myself and just allowing me to be me around you. Even if that person confuses the heck out of both of us.

For Mercy Rogers. You continue to be a light in my life. Thank you for being there and supporting my career along the way.

A special thanks to Ryan Welsh, Thomas Fitzgerald, Buff Faye, and Carol Roth for words of encouragement and support in general.

Finally, to my readers who are either new or are joining me from the *Between Heaven and Hell* series. Thank you for picking up this novel.

ABOUT THE AUTHOR

L A Michaels is a Michigan native growing up in the Rochester Hills, Troy, Lake Orion areas. They currently live in Warren. L A has also lived in Wichita, Kansas, and Rock Hill, South Carolina, over a two-year period during their teenage years. An avid reader, soap opera fan, comic book fan, and history buff.

Follow L A Michaels on the following platforms:
Instagram: lamichaelsauthor
Twitter: lamichaels1995
Facebook: L A Michaels
GoodReads: L.A. Michaels

Follow the cover artist "LuviiiLove" on their DeviantArt page as well!